HOLDING PUTTER

5/13/19

To Nancy –

May you enjoy reading Holding

Putter.

John C.H. Lefler

JOHN C.H. LEFLER

WESTBOW
PRESS®
A DIVISION OF THOMAS NELSON
& ZONDERVAN

Scripture quotations are from the Revised Standard Version of the Bible, copyright © 1946, 1952, and 1971 the Division of Christian Education of the National Council of the Churches of Christ in the United States of America. Used by permission. All rights reserved.

This is a work of fiction. All of the characters, names, incidents, organizations, and dialogue in this novel are either the products of the author's imagination or are used fictitiously.

WestBow Press books may be ordered through booksellers or by contacting:

WestBow Press
A Division of Thomas Nelson & Zondervan
1663 Liberty Drive
Bloomington, IN 47403
www.westbowpress.com
1 (866) 928-1240

Because of the dynamic nature of the Internet, any web addresses or links contained in this book may have changed since publication and may no longer be valid. The views expressed in this work are solely those of the author and do not necessarily reflect the views of the publisher, and the publisher hereby disclaims any responsibility for them.

Any people depicted in stock imagery provided by Getty Images are models, and such images are being used for illustrative purposes only. Certain stock imagery © Getty Images.

ISBN: 978-1-9736-4291-6 (sc)
ISBN: 978-1-9736-4292-3 (hc)
ISBN: 978-1-9736-4290-9 (e)

Library of Congress Control Number: 2018912271

Print information available on the last page.

WestBow Press rev. date: 10/18/2018

CONTENTS

Section II Later Life

DEDICATION

To Annabeal, my beloved wife whose combined encouragement and support made this book possible.

To Wesley, my lifelong brother and friend, and in memory of Sammy, who did his dead level best.

To God be the glory.

PROLOGUE

There were times in America's good old days when times were not so good. In the rural south during the mid-1900s, conditions were harsh. Job opportunities were scarce. Money was tight. Tempers were short, and most folks couldn't make a decent living. The young nation had overcome two World Wars, the Dust Bowl, and a Depression. But times were changing. In the North Carolina foothills, textile mills were springing up, and cotton was king. Furniture companies began to flourish. Tobacco farmers were making ends meet. Some were getting rich. Seasonal crops like grains, vegetables, and dairy products were pumping America's food supply chain.

Into this setting was placed a rural Methodist minister, his wife—a Bible teacher—and their three sons, Junior, Jake, and Sammy. At an early age Sammy, with no known cause or cure, was faced with what was to become a debilitating lifelong handicap.

In the days that followed, there were few rewards for parenting a handicapped child. Mainly there were disappointments and sacrifices, with slivers of successes and satisfaction along the way. But woven into the humble lives of this family of five were some stories worth telling and some memories worth preserving.

SECTION I

THE EARLY YEARS

CHAPTER 1

THE PROBLEM

In the late 1930s, Reverend and Mrs. Bain Wesley Lamb served at three small Methodist churches in the foothills of the North Carolina mountains. Recently out of college, they were a hopeful, happy, struggling family. The Lambs had two young sons: Bain Wesley Lamb Jr. and his younger brother, Francis Samuel Lamb, who was nicknamed Sammy by his brother at an early age. Jake, who some said was an afterthought, was to come along ten years later.

When Sammy was four, his mother was the first to notice that he would occasionally drift off into a blank stare. He wouldn't respond to his name. Sometimes he couldn't be shaken free from a strange "deep sleep," as his mama first referred to it. Instinctively she knew that Sammy's actions were not normal, and soon she insisted on seeking medical attention. The closest city for an expert medical opinion was in Charlotte. Apprehensive, the little family drove solemnly on poorly maintained country roads until they neared the city. The preliminary end-of-day medical results were not encouraging.

After a full regimen of testing, one pediatrician thought Sammy might have some rare form of amnesia. Another general practitioner surmised it might be an "overly sensitive and overprotective mother not familiar with the intricacies of child rearing." A third opinion suggested that Sammy might grow out of it, and the family was advised to keep a record of his "spells" and come back for further testing, if needed.

By the time Sammy was ready to go to school, nothing had really improved, and it became obvious that his mental and physical skills were limited at best. Preacher, as he was called by most of the folks who knew him, and Mama decided it would be best to withhold him from the public school system. It was an easy decision since the schools in their area made no special provisions for children with learning disabilities.

Generally speaking, life continued as best it could. The family was moved by the Methodist Conference to another rural appointment near the town of Cherryville—and closer to Charlotte.

Mama held a college degree in Bible studies and English literature, and she found a part-time substitute teaching position in the public schools. Having both parents working outside the home was uncommon, but Preacher was willing to share childcare responsibilities when Mama was substituting at school.

Preacher was loving and kind, as could be expected, since he was a member of the clergy. He also had a no-nonsense side, a side where people who really knew him dared not to venture.

The preacher was about as well known for his gardening as he was for his preaching. When he was a boy he grew up on a 151-acre North Carolina farm where farming meant survival in every respect. Consequently, whether Preacher lived in the city or the country, he found a way to grow food for his family.

Preacher also saw himself not only as the primary provider for the family but also its protector, as his father had been. In all circumstances, Preacher's leadership manner perfectly fit the biblical mold of the man being the head of the household. In certain situations that meant by necessity that Preacher was all business.

Late one Saturday afternoon, Preacher asked Junior to go to the garden with him to assist in staking some tomato plants. They had no sooner begun when they heard a car rattling down their driveway. Sammy was playing by himself in his sandbox between the driveway and the garden, which was where he normally played when there was gardening to be done.

As the preacher and Junior watched from about a stone's throw away, the car came to an abrupt stop, the passenger door opened, and an overall-clad stranger jumped out, picked up Sammy, who was kicking and screaming, and shoved him into the back seat of the car. Preacher sprang like a wildcat, and before anyone could make any sense out of anything, he attacked the car and anyone in the front seat by smashing the front windshield with the blunt end of his seven-foot hickory tomato stake. In less than the blink of an eye, he flipped the weapon around in a half baton twirl move, and now with an open access to the front seat passenger, he pointed the end of the stob directly toward the stunned man who had abducted Sammy. The next sound that came from the vehicle was a surprised scream from Sammy's abductor. Preacher's perfectly timed spear stopped inches before piercing the kidnapper's left shoulder.

"Don't move!" Preacher warned. He deliberately withdrew his weapon and circled the hood of the car. "Now I'm going to get you!" Preacher threatened as he glared squarely into the face of the driver. If Preacher even thought that he might be met face-to-face with a pistol, he never showed any reluctance or hesitation to attack.

"Here's yer boy," the driver bargained, grabbing Sammy and pulling him from the backseat. Holding the child by his shirt, the driver heaved Sammy out the door. As he slammed his door in Preacher's face the not-to-be-outdone stranger pointed his finger and yelled at Preacher, "You mind this. We'll get you. We'll be back and get you good for this!"

"We'll see about that!" Preacher shouted back.

It could have been Sammy's flying through the air and tumbling in fear and tears on the ground, or it might have been the kidnapper's threat, but Preacher responded with a ferocious, guttural outcry that resembled a bear's roar before an attack.

"You won't be getting me or my boy. If ever you believed in praying, you better start right now, brother."

With no more ado, Preacher used the dull end of his weapon again to shatter the driver's window pane. It was then he heard the driver's soulful plea.

"Please, Lord, don't let him hit me in my good eye. Mister, we ain't never coming back. I swear. Never. We ain't never goin' to see you again."

Preacher slowly withdrew his spear, looked across the front seat, and added,

"I don't know who you two are or why you tried to take my boy, but you are two lucky men. If I were not a preacher of the gospel, only the good Lord knows what would have happened to you."

In the next few anxious moments, the driver was able to get his stalled Ford coupe started, and with dust pouring and gravel spitting from the rear tires, the visitors were forever gone up and out of the driveway.

Preacher turned to Junior, whose eyes were as wide as his forehead, "Son, you better take Sammy back to the house. I've got to finish staking those plants before dark."

"Yes, sir," Junior said in awe with a newfound respect for his father. "Daddy, should we call the sheriff?" Junior wondered.

"I'll call him later. And tell Mama I'll be there soon for supper."

Years later when someone asked Preacher if the story about the encounter with the kidnappers was true, Preacher said, "The Lord has a way of taking care of his people, and I have a way of taking care of mine."

CHAPTER 2

A NEIGHBOR

In farm country there are few, if any, next-door neighbors, and Sammy depended mostly upon Junior, Preacher, and Mama for companionship. Twice in the past few months, Sammy's seizures had returned. The first time Mama thought it might have been brought on by an unusually high fever. But when it happened several weeks later, the family made another trip to the medical center in Charlotte. After a battery of expensive tests, the physician asked the boy a curious question.

"Ever stick anything up your nose, Sammy?"

After some thought, Sammy said, "I might have stuck a seed in there one time."

"Which side?" Sammy pointed toward his left nostril.

"What kind of seed?"

"A little one."

"How little?"

"Oh, maybe this big." Sammy pointed to his smallest left hand fingernail. The doctor looked at Mama, then to Preacher for enlightenment. They were puzzled.

"I think it might have been a cherry seed," Sammy confessed. Mama was dumbfounded.

"When, Francie?" she asked, the name she often called him when he was a little boy.

"When, son?" the preacher inquired.

"Maybe when I was little."

Dr. Yow's fingers pressed upon Sammy's cheeks, then crawled toward Sammy's left eye, moving gently but with certainty upward to Sammy's temple. "Any pain?"

"No, sir."

After a moment's thought, Dr. Yow turned toward Mama and Preacher. "The seed might have migrated near his brain," he surmised. "Now this isn't a diagnosis, just a guess, but it's possible, I suppose, that when Sammy turns to a certain position, the brain responds accordingly to the pressure applied by the foreign object. If his condition worsens in any way, bring him back, and we will follow up on my theory."

With that devastating news Preacher Lamb and his family made their way to the door. "No charge for today," the doctor added. "I expect you all are going to need a break every chance you get."

Three days later Sammy was invited to go up to see their next-door neighbor Miss Mamie, as he called her. Mamie Connor was his Sunday school teacher, and she lived on a working farm with her husband, Hoyt, and son, Joseph David, who happened to be Junior's best friend.

Sammy loved going to Miss Mamie's because when he was there, she devoted 100 percent of her time to his needs. Always she would begin by reading to him. On his last visit Miss Mamie selected A. A. Milne's poem "Jonathan Jo Has a Mouth Like an O," which made Sammy laugh.

"What do you want me to read to you today?" she asked.

"Oh, Miss Mamie, I want to hear one of your poems about Slim Sam." Slim Sam was an imaginary little boy created in poetry by Miss Mamie. Her intended goal was for Sammy to think of himself as she read about Sam—a little fellow who would often get into trouble even when he tried to do the right thing … just like Sammy was sometimes prone to do.

"Let me see. It's right here," she began. "This one is called, 'Poor Slim Sam Flim-flam-i-gen.'"

> One day Slim's neighbor, Old Mr. Cobb
>
> Said, "Son have you ever tried your hand at a job?'
>
> "No, sir," said Sam. His head turned with a jerk.
>
> "I've always been scared of doin' hard work."

Sammy smiled. Mamie continued.

> Mr. Cobb told Sam, "Workin's not too hard.
>
> You can do a few chores or mow someone's yard."

"I know," said Sam, "it's not one bit funny

To try to get by without any money.

And to tell you the truth, and I really can't lie,

There's nothin' that nothin' ever can buy.

I know what I'll do. A mower I'll borrow,

And I'll do it right now...or maybe tomorrow."

"Miss Mamie do you think I could ever get a job?" Sammy inquired.

"Of course you could. Why, just the other day Mr. Connor and I were talking about how we needed somebody to pick that little patch of cotton over yonder in the shade. Later on this evenin' it should be cool enough for you to pick a batch. I'll make you a little sack from a small pillowcase, stitch a strap on it so you can sling it over your shoulder, and why we'll call it your cotton-pickin' poke."

For the next two hours Miss Mamie cut and sewed. Finally she said, "I think that it's cool enough now. Are you ready? I'll show you what to do. This bag is all you'll need, and I'll pay you ten cents a poke."

No one had ever gone to work with a better attitude than Sammy did. By day's end his fingertips were scraped and pricked by the cotton bolls. Specks of dried blood dotted his fingers. When it was time for Sammy to go home, Miss Mamie came out with a jug of lemonade, a few cookies, and a pocket full of coins. "How many bags did you pick, Sammy?"

"Eight!" he proclaimed.

"Do you know how much I owe you?"

"No, ma'am," he said.

"I owe you eighty cents," she exclaimed and began to count out a quarter, two dimes, four nickels, and fifteen pennies.

Sammy looked at all the money, and with a partial smile and teary eyes, he turned to his grown-up friend, and said, "Thank-you, Miss Mamie. This is the proudest day of my life, and this time I am proud of me."

An unprecedented December snowfall came with a fury that year. Fifteen inches of snow fell over a three-day period. The Lambs had a surprise, too. Mama gave birth to their third son named Jacob Christian, whom they nicknamed Jake. Mama, who was modest beyond reason, kept her pregnancy a secret from her parents and her brothers and sisters until the baby arrived. Due to the weather, the driving conditions on the streets and highways were so treacherous that the baby could not be brought home until three days before Christmas. The Lambs said that baby Jake was the only gift they needed because he was a gift from God. Preacher was almost fifty, and Mama was forty-five.

With the weather improving, the family decided to drive to Mama's parents' home for Christmas, which was their tradition. Mama called her parents to give them the news of the baby's birth and to announce their plans to be together with on Christmas Day. Nannie and Papa were in their eighties and always the life of their party. When they heard the news of another new baby, they were ecstatic. Two of Mama's younger sisters had already had babies within the last twelve months, and no one even suspected that Mama, at her age, would have another child.

Nannie assured Mama that there was certainly room for one more, especially new baby Jake. Since most of Mama's six siblings had children of their own, thirty-five or forty family members were expected to gather for the day.

Christmas was always special for everyone present, but there was a tinge of sadness that prevailed. That year three of the family members were away serving overseas in World War II. The remaining men who were at home followed their annual tradition of walking the land hunting quail or stalking the banks of Rocky River hoping for a shot at a passing duck.

The women gathered in the open kitchen and dining room areas setting up for the afternoon Christmas meal. Everyone brought their favorite covered dishes, and as always, there was a huge turkey with dressing and noodles. In the process the sisters and nieces visited, trying to catch up with a year's news. Baby Jake was a center of attention.

In the yard the boys had their sleds and made the best of the remaining snow. Meanwhile Sammy watched. After the covered dish feast, the family gathered in the hallway beside the piano to sing Christmas carols. Every voice tried to out-sing the other. Sammy's off-key notes could be heard above the rest. He was typically about a half-note behind, attempting to mimic their words.

By 4:30 the children led the pack into the living room, and before a roaring fire and a ten-foot, fully lighted and decorated Christmas tree came the exchange and opening of packages. Sammy received five gifts that he would treasure for a lifetime. Mama and Preacher gave him a harmonica, which he blew almost daily for the next fifty years. Aunt Dovie didn't have children, and the nieces and nephews became her kids. As a result, her gifts were always highly anticipated and appreciated. That year she gave Sammy a Hopalong Cassidy set of binoculars. Nannie and Papa's gift was their customary silver dollar, which was saved and never spent. Sammy loved and collected keys, so Junior surprised him with a key to the house, which thereafter could always and forever be found in Sammy's left pants pocket. Finally, Uncle P. O. gave him a handmade ring fashioned from an Indian-head nickel, which P. O. had made for him during his U. S. Navy deployment on a battleship in the Pacific during World War II. It was Sammy's best and most memorable Christmas ever.

Sammy proudly gave Mama and Preacher a brilliant green hobnail ashtray he had picked out and purchased with some of his cotton-pickin' money. Of course, neither parent smoked, but they knew that Sammy loved green, and they decided to keep it prominently displayed on a shelf in their living room. At day's end, reluctant good-byes were said, and the families made their way home. Sammy played his harmonica. It was the sign of a good day.

CHAPTER 3

A CRISIS

In North Carolina and throughout the South there were constant reminders of the Civil War, or the War Between the States, which southerners preferred it to be called. Scattered among the farms were outcroppings of shanty homes almost exclusively occupied by "colored folks." Within view of the parsonage were two such communities named Gibsonville. Every day about dusk several colored families would walk up the road past the parsonage, and Sammy would be waiting to say hello. Color was never an obstacle for him or for any member of the Lamb family. In fact, Mrs. Lamb had been asked on frequent occasions to substitute teach in the nearby all-colored school—John Chavis High School.

One day an elder member of the passersby asked Sammy if Preacher was at home. Sammy hurried as best he could to find his dad, and in a moment the two men were talking.

"I'm Bishop Ebenezer Hardin, and I pastor the Belfont AME Church. It's been suggested by a few of my members that we ask you to preach at our homecoming service in three weeks. We start at eleven o'clock and pretty much make a day of it," he said with a wide smile.

With no hesitation, Preacher said he would be there. Twenty-one days later in their best Sunday clothes, Mama, Junior, and Sammy were escorted down to the front row, and Preacher joined Bishop Hardin in the pulpit. Baby Jake was held by his occasional babysitter, Miss Angelina. The opening singing, all spirituals, lasted for over an hour. After lengthy announcements and prayer, the bishop called upon Reverend Lamb to preach. The sermon title was "Moses, Free from Bondage."

Preacher read selected verses from the book of Exodus about Moses's life story, beginning with his unusual birth hiding in the bulrushes, to murdering an aggressive Hebrew slave master, and eventually becoming a mighty leader with successes and disappointments.

Preacher paused, looked around the congregation, and spoke. "Moses was a man *handpicked by God.*"

"Yes, he was," came a response from the congregation.

Immediately, Preacher embraced the responsive nature of his congregation, and the remainder of his message was intentionally presented to encourage a dialogue exchange. Being a naturally gifted raconteur, Preacher welcomed the congregation's participation.

"*God* said *my people, my people* have been in bondage four hundred long years. *It's time to be free. It's time to go home!*"

"Amen, Preacher. Yes, it is time."

"It won't be easy, children."

"No, Lord, not easy."

"*We will see great miracles.*"

"Praise you, Jesus. Praise you."

"And we'll struggle in the wilderness."

"Preach it, Pastor. Preach on."

"But the God of all gods said *we will prevail!*"

"Yes, Lord. We'll get there someday, Lord. Someday."

For the next hour the Preacher preached, and his congregation responded as if Belfont AME church members and the Israelites were in interchangeable roles. Following the service, the family feasted on a covered dish meal like none other. The Lambs and the Hardins had become good friends.

It was around midnight three days later when Sammy ran into the bedroom. "I hear somebody outside."

In the front yard were a dozen or more white-clad figures, hooded, appearing like strange, ghostly apparitions behind a burning cross. Preacher reached for his sawed-off shotgun behind the bedroom door. Then another thought came to mind. He slowly walked out the front door to meet the mob unarmed, face-to-face. A few in the crowd began taunting. Preacher raised both arms. The mob quieted.

"Men of this community," he began. "I know why you are here. I know why you are upset. But I also imagine that if you removed your coverings, I would recognize many or most of you. I would think that some of you are members of my church directly behind your backs. Just remember that the cross you are burning tonight in this yard is the same cross you honor when you step into the church doors. It is the cross of Jesus, who himself died to cover sins like the one you are committing right now. Now go on home and be with your families. They need you to protect them from harm and danger as I am protecting my family now."

15

Slowly the crowd silently disbanded. Preacher went back inside.

"That's why I love you. You are a good man, Bain," Mama said. "A very good man."

"Were you scared, Daddy?" Sammy inquired.

"I was concerned, son, but sometimes I do get scared."

"Why didn't you get scared?" Sammy wondered.

"Tonight I was fairly confident that I knew most of those folks. They were neighbors who in their hearts didn't want to hurt us but got worked up by one or two bullies who didn't have the nerve to attack us alone. And I felt assured that God was on our side."

"Like Moses did, Daddy?"

"Yes, son. Like Moses did."

"Daddy, you always know what to do." Then from out of nowhere Sammy said, "Do you think I will ever be normal?"

"I hope so. We all hope so, but for now you are normal enough. You are just fine."

"But I'm a little bit afraid," the boy said. "Can I sleep with you and Mama tonight?"

"Anytime you are afraid, you can always crawl in bed with us."

In the back bedroom Junior and little brother, Jake, were sound asleep, totally unaware that this night had been like none other.

CHAPTER 4

THE BURDEN

Mama's never-ceasing concern would not go away. Preacher felt it, too. The aunts and uncles and even Nannie and Papa slowly began to realize in futility that there was no cure. Like a persistent cough, Sammy's condition was not improving as everyone hoped. Only once a doctor raised faint hopes when he suggested the boy "might grow out of it." But this sickness, malady, illness, condition, whatever it was, was a diabolical foe. No one even knew what to call it. No one was willing to project future outcomes. No one knew. No one.

As a result of Mama's patient and determined instruction, Sammy could slowly read simple sentences. He could print the alphabet in capital letters, although some letters were backward. He liked his name, Sammy, because each of the letters except the S looked the same whether he printed them forward or backward. His vocabulary had not expanded beyond a basic conversational level. Some words he consistently mispronounced and could not correct. Exactly became eggsjactly. Horse was whores. Library was iberry. Butter became budder. Not surprisingly, he also had diminishing motor skills. Sammy wobbled uneasily when he walked. He occasionally needed to hold out his arms to maintain his balance. Attempts at running invariably ended with him tripping and falling.

Although there are normal physical changes when one enters the teens, Sammy's changes were unorthodox. His knuckles and ears became somewhat enlarged. His fingernails were bitten into the quick, and his teeth became a dingy, dull off-white. Even with all the abnormalities, Sammy was not a major distraction in public, but he was different, and people noticed and usually looked away.

If and when he had a seizure, he would fall, and a small cluster of onlookers would gather. A family member would bolster his head and neck, applying firm but gentle direct pressure or massage. Occasionally, a volunteer would offer to assist, if needed. Slowly the crowd would disperse. Sammy would gradually regain his senses, and the family would move on.

Mama and Preacher prayed faithfully for a miracle cure. Mama especially needed peer support, but being somewhat isolated out in the country with no extended family except Miss Mamie to lean on, she had no other friend upon whom she could depend to lend a sympathetic ear.

One day when she and Mamie were together Mama said, "Sammy wants to go to school."

In disbelief the two friends stared at each other, shaking their heads. Finally, Miss Mamie suggested that they begin a search for a school, a clinic, a handicapped support group, something, anything that might contribute to Sammy's developmental progress. After several months of looking, their research turned up nothing.

One day Mama said, "Sammy what do you like, and what makes you happy?"

"Chocolate pie," he thoughtfully began, "and ice cream and fried chicken and going to Nannie and Papas, and playing my harmonica, seeing Miss Mamie, my binoculars, gospel music, ball games, my birthday, and Christmas."

"And what would you like to do that you haven't done before?"

He thought. "See the ocean. Maybe go to school, and," then he whispered, "have a girlfriend like other boys."

"Francis Samuel Lamb, you better watch that!" They both laughed.

CHAPTER 5

WHEEZER

Rumors had been floating around for weeks concerning someone from out of town buying old man Gantt's place on Buffalo Creek. Boss Gantt kept mostly to himself for a lifetime. By day he ran a sawmill. By night he had another job. Most folks knew that he had been dealing in an illegal liquor business and probably was making his own moonshine for sale. Cars would slip into his driveway late at night, turn off their headlights, and slowly creep down the road to his house. A dim light would appear at the door, then disappear for a few moments. The door would reopen, a brown bag and some money would be exchanged, and the house would go dark again.

Federal agents tried time and again to trap him making a sale without ever being able to make an arrest. Just before he died, he made a deal with a real estate broker to sell all 288 acres of his land for $150,000 to an out-of- state buyer. He then willed all the proceeds from the sale to his girlfriend, leaving his only son out in the cold completely. When Boss Gantt died from liver damage, some in the community thought, *Good riddance.*

Gantt's only kin was his son, Wheezer, who was as nearly worthless as a human being could be. He never went to school for any extended period of time and was kicked out more times than anyone cared to count. The last time was because he was caught on the schoolyard with a dozen or more green frogs. Grabbing two at a time, he pulled them out of his pocket and bit off their heads just to hear the girls scream.

Wheezer always wore a silver skull ring on his middle finger. It had emerald green eyes. The ring matched his personality perfectly and was his calling card. One day the owners of Hudson Hardware in town saw him slipping out of the store with a baseball glove under his jacket. Dock Hudson, the owner, called him out and threatened to get the police if he didn't surrender the glove. Wheezer walked right up to him and spat a mouthful of Brown's Mule chewing tobacco spit directly into Mr. Hudson's face. In the commotion, Wheezer intentionally allowed the glove to slide from his coat to the floor, then kicked it underneath a table. He opened his coat, revealing nothing, called Mr. Hudson a liar, threw up his ring finger in Mr. Hudson's face, and left.

Wheezer was furious when he was told what his father had done with the land. With no place to live Wheezer became a wanderer, moving from barn to barn to vacant building to any deserted, unlocked shelter he could find.

One day he was shuffling down the road past the parsonage when Sammy saw him going by. Although he didn't know Wheezer, Sammy never met a stranger and threw up his hand, said hello, and started toward him. Wheezer turned toward Sammy, glared at him, and then stuck up his middle finger, displaying his green-eyed skull ring. Sammy then stuck up his middle finger, proudly displaying his World War II Christmas ring from Uncle P. O.

Stunned and amazed by the gesture, Wheezer was momentarily speechless but caught himself in time to stick up both fists, walk toward Sammy, and shove him to the ground. Apparently a gene from Preacher's side of the family was aroused, because one thing Sammy wasn't was a coward. He popped up from the ground, and probably the last thing Wheezer expected was Sammy's left-handed uppercut, which barely grazed Wheezer's chin but smashed directly into Wheezer's somewhat prominent nose. Dazed and in disbelief, Wheezer retreated. Sammy turned and walked away but checked to make sure Wheezer wasn't coming up from behind. Some things Sammy was prone to forget, but he would not forget the vindictive look on Wheezer's face glaring at him from the driveway.

"What on earth happened to you, son?" Mama asked.

"Wheezer Gantt shoved me to the ground, and I got up and cold cocked him."

"Cold cocked? Wherever did you learn that language?"

"I dunno. I guess I heard it from somebody at church."

Mama checked outside to make sure Wheezer was okay, but he was nowhere to be seen. For a moment Mama imagined that Sammy was almost becoming a typical fifteen-year-old. Two hours later he had his most severe seizure in months.

CHAPTER 6

EMOTIONS

The new owners of Boss Gantt's place were the Gastons—James, his wife, Amy, and their teenage daughter, Della. They had sold their farm implements business near Ocala, Florida, to start anew in the cooler North Carolina climate. Long before they moved to their new surroundings, they began clearing the land, building a new house, sowing Kentucky bluegrass pasture seeds by the sackfuls, and installing impressive white fencing around what was to become Carolina Stables.

The entire pasturing project had been delayed by over a month while Federal Department of Revenue agents scoured the land after one of the state's largest liquor stills was accidentally unearthed by the construction workers. The still was located beneath a prominent and overtly obvious brush pile on what had been Boss and Wheezer Gantt's land.

It may have never been discovered, but the brush pile was being routinely bulldozed so the new owners could clear an area for a spring-fed fishpond. With the stumps and limbs pushed away, it was apparent that the debris had only been piled there to give the appearance of being burned periodically. In retrospect, the debris had never been consumed by fire. For years smoke from the underground brewing chamber had filtered through the brush heap, giving the appearance of a brush fire with no one the wiser.

An unusually wet summer season had also contributed to delaying the construction of the Gastons' new ranch-style home, and it wasn't until autumn that the Gastons were actually able to move permanently onto the new property. It was a welcomed move since their temporary apartment in Shelby was barely large enough for the three of them from the beginning, and with the passage of time, they increasingly felt the need for more space.

Shortly after the Gastons settled in their new house, Amy Gaston and Della stopped by the parsonage to get acquainted with the Lamb family.

While Mrs. Gaston and Mama visited, Della, Sammy, and Jake sat on the front porch playing Chinese checkers. Della was a beautiful, petite, polite, and well-spoken teenager. With dark blue eyes and long auburn hair, Della was striking to say the least. Since early childhood, her primary passion was her father's horses, and when she was not in school, she spent every available hour either riding or grooming every quarter horse in the stables.

Preacher and Junior had been out making calls, which was Preacher's term for visiting his parishioners. When they arrived back at the parsonage, Junior was the first to reach the porch. He stopped abruptly in his tracks and took a long look at Della. Della smiled. That instant changed Junior's life forever. She was by far the prettiest girl he had ever seen. At age seventeen, Junior was en route to falling in love.

Junior's magical moment was interrupted when with little or no warning, Sammy had one of his seizures. Preacher and Junior rushed to his aid. Although it was not as violent as some, it was enough to frighten the Gastons, especially Della, and they promptly excused themselves, offering to come back again when it was more convenient. In frustration Mama called the clinic in Charlotte again, and Sammy, who was beginning to dread the appointments, was scheduled to see a neurologist the following week.

Unfortunately, the appointment was of very little practical value in determining a cause of the seizures. It was suggested that emotional situations might be triggering a stressful reaction, and Sammy should try to avoid any activity that might induce stress. Since the seizures were becoming more frequent than in the past, the doctor recommended beginning Sammy on a mild dosage of phenobarbital, a medication often used to minimize or prevent epilepsy or seizures in children. The family returned home with mixed emotions, as usual.

CHAPTER 7

CHANGING TIMES

For years Junior had been trying to find a way to buy a horse. Always the problem had been too little money and too few available horses. With the opening of Carolina Stables, half of his problem had been resolved. Growing up as a farm boy, Preacher had also wanted his son to have a horse, not a pony, but a horse, a strong horse so that he could ride it too. In fact, Preacher offered to pay half the purchase price as an incentive, if Junior could find the right horse and would agree to pay for the other half and provide feed from his own money.

The Lambs were blessed to live in a mineral-rich section of the state, and the multiple uses for mica were still being discovered. For a part-time job with the flexible hours that Junior needed, the area mica mines provided the most likely opportunities for his employment.

Junior was hearty, strong, and dependable, and he had no trouble securing an after-school job. He was also given the option for full-time summer hours, if he desired. It was dirty, hot work, but Junior was highly motivated. The job was providing money to buy a horse and feed. Of greater value to him was the chance to share horses as a common interest with Della and her family.

In its raw form mica was located in dense outcroppings. In nature, it was formed in paper-thin transparent sheets, each sheet sturdy enough to resist crumbling but rigid enough to break when direct pressure was applied. Usually its appearance was clear, nearly transparent. Occasionally, it had a smoky, pink, or green tint, which was marketable for the production of costume jewelry. The most promising future use, although speculative, was in the production of computer chips. For commercial exploitation it was an idea being developed ten years before its time.

Within a mile or two from the parsonage was the Phoenix mine, an excavation over one hundred feet in depth and three hundred feet in diameter. It was dangerous since it was partially filled with rain and runoff water. Also, there was no security fencing to keep a careless observer from falling over the edge into the abyss and almost certain death. From the pit had been extracted thousands of tons of raw mica, which after being graded for purity and color, was then shipped globally to processors and manufacturers.

In the three months that followed, Junior worked from daybreak until dusk in the mine. As a result, with his own money he was able to purchase Daisy, a beautiful chestnut mare with a perfect diamond blaze and blond highlights on her tail and mane. Mr. Gaston was a pleasure to do business with and even agreed to allow Daisy to board for free at their farm until a suitable stable could be constructed behind the parsonage.

Junior was in no hurry to bring Daisy home but went by the Gaston farm every day to see Della, and Daisy too. Soon they were riding the trails between their two homes, and they became familiar faces in each other's households.

Since Sammy had begun taking medication for his attacks, he had become more lethargic. He slept longer hours and spent even more of his waking hours on the front porch playing his harmonica, practicing shooting a slingshot Junior had made for him from the limb of a dogwood tree, playing board games with Jake, and looking through his binoculars for hours on end.

In fact, Sammy became quite observant. With help from family members, he learned to identify some birds by name. He learned to distinguish the most common trees by their general appearance and the shapes of their leaves. Mama particularly was pleased that through the help of his binoculars, Sammy was slowly developing an inquisitive mind. She decided that for Christmas a more adult set might make a perfect surprise under the tree.

CHAPTER 8

MR. SAMMY

One of Sammy's other outlets was listening to the vintage Zenith floor model radio that was in the living room. Although there were only a limited number of radio stations available without becoming washed out by static, Sammy would listen to music he could accompany somewhat with his harmonica. Weekend ball games found him riveted to the speaker for hours on end. Even the newscasts kept his attention. Soap operas, *Amos and Andy*, and cowboy serials wrapped up his listening favorites.

The top of his list of favorite programs belonged to Renfro Valley Folks, a country music and gospel broadcast brought live from the hills of Mt. Vernon, Kentucky. At the beginning of each week's program Sammy would join the announcer in opening each show with, "And now friends by the way of the magic carpet of radio, we take you to the old barn in Renfro Valley ..."

As a result of radio expanding his universe, the family recognized that Sammy was becoming a fanatic of absolutes in his opinions. In short, there were never any "maybes" in his life, only "yeses, nos, likes, and dislikes."

For example, Sammy liked: Gospel music, Methodists, Americans, the Yankees, Duke, chocolate, blonds, Democrats, Oldsmobiles, and hymns. By contrast, he did not like: Russians, the Dodgers, Notre Dame, vanilla, redheads, Fords, Republicans, or jazz. As a result of his predictable opinions, he became the target of relentless teasing. Even Jake took advantage of his vulnerabilities. Mama would do her best to protect Sammy, but invariably an opportunity would arise.

"Sammy," Junior would begin, "if you had a choice of a girlfriend between a girl who was a pretty Democrat redhead or a beautiful, blond Republican which one would you choose?"

"Neither one!" would be his immediate response.

Never was there hesitation.

"Hopalong Cassidy or Roy Rogers?"

Immediately, "Both!" He liked all cowboys.

And so it was, for better or worse, a pattern of absolutes were implanted for a lifetime. Day after day those obvious likes and dislikes were a gentle form of teasing that he enjoyed as much as his friendly tormentors.

Another deviation that could guarantee a predictable reaction would begin with anyone saying something like, "Sammy, would you rather watch Duke play basketball or Sammy Snead play golf?" He would always pause momentarily because anything with Sammy in it would grab his attention.

"Duke," would be his certain reply. "I don't like golf."

Sammy was often willing to try almost anything at least once, and he was rarely certain if he was going to be happy or disappointed with the unknown outcome.

Junior had held a driver's license for almost two years, and Preacher had great confidence in his son's driving ability allowing him to use the family car, a 1947 Oldsmobile, whenever it was available. One afternoon Mama asked Junior to run to the store to get sugar for a pie she was making. As usual, Sammy said, "Can I go?" Before they pulled out of the driveway, Junior noticed that a group of the Gibsonville folks from the Belfont AME Church were walking down the road.

"Sammy," he said, "would you like to learn how to drive?"

"Yes! I would like it, but I don't know how, and I might get sick," Sammy replied.

"For today we'll just practice. You sit in the driver's seat, and I will sit toward the middle so I can control the steering wheel and the pedals."

It sounded like a workable plan to Sammy, so he slid over to the driver's seat.

"Roll down your window, and be sure to wave and blow the horn if we see anyone," Junior advised.

The sleek, black Olds wheeled out of the driveway, and down the road they went. Big brother allowed the car to slow down as they approached the walkers. Sammy waved and blew the horn as they navigated through the group.

"That's Mr. Sammy drivin' that car!" Angelina yelled.

Soon the Lamb brothers were out of sight, but within five minutes they had completed their shopping at the store and were on the way home when Junior spotted the walkers up ahead. This time he sped up a bit and told Sammy to blow the horn and wave again. The road cleared, and as they sped by, Bishop Hardin's stare focused on the driver. Sammy waved as if he were leading the Rose Bowl Parade. After a few minutes the bishop's church family approached the parsonage and walked up the driveway. Junior and Sammy casually went down to meet them, but Junior feared that maybe the bishop was going report to Preacher that Sammy had been driving. Instead, the bishop's son, Uriah, flashed the biggest smile Sammy had ever seen.

"Mr. Sammy, Mr. Sammy," he said, "we saw you comin' down the road, and you sho can drive."

Sammy glowed inside. It was the first time anyone had called him mister, and he thought to himself, *I am growing up.*

In a way, Sammy was physically growing up, but in his intellectual development, the outlook was not promising.

CHAPTER 9

A FAMILY ADDITION

One morning Mama opened the back door to see an unexpected visitor. "My, oh my, what have I found here?" she asked herself, loud enough for the family to hear.

Mama stooped down and gently picked up the tiniest tan chihuahua she had ever seen. It was shivering and obviously malnourished. Upon closer inspection, it appeared that both front legs had been damaged, and perhaps it was in the early stages of glaucoma, at least one eye appeared to be slightly opaque.

"What is that thing?" Preacher began.

"A baby dog. Mama, I've never had a dog. I want that puppy. Daddy, can we keep it?"

"No, no, no, no, no, no, no!" Preacher declared as he looked over Mama's shoulder. "It's not a puppy. That animal is sick. Too sick to be outside, and we have never allowed an animal to live inside the parsonage. Why, the church's parsonage committee would pitch a fit if they even thought it was here. And it probably has fleas to boot," he said.

"This is no puppy," Mama agreed. "He's turning a bit gray around the muzzle. He's not wearing a collar. I bet someone dumped him. But look at that face and those markings. As pitiful as he is, he has the lines of a champion."

At that moment Sammy began the stare, which foretold another seizure could be forthcoming. He moaned.

"Just what we need," Preacher blurted, "another handicapped body in this family."

Before the words were off his lips, Preacher knew he had said the wrong thing.

"Bain!" Mama screamed.

Preacher had never seen that look of disgust and disappointment on his wife's face. He had never heard that tone in her voice. But her eyes—her eyes spoke a thousand words in a split second, and none of those silent words were good. Unfortunately, Sammy had not lost total consciousness either, and he heard the words come out of his Daddy's mouth—ten words that he didn't need to hear coming from his father: "Just what we need, another handicapped body in this house."

In that smallest of split seconds, Preacher had sown a seed, a seed of unworthiness, between him and his son that lingered with Sammy for years. Sammy began to cry.

Holding the dog in one arm and Sammy in the other, Mama said, "We are keeping this dog. This dog stays right here, and that's that … and tonight after he's had a bath, he is sleeping in bed with me."

Preacher started to speak but thought better of it. He had already said too much.

"What are we going to name him, Mama?" Sammy wondered.

"I don't know, son," she said. "We'll see. If he's like most pets, he'll find a way to name himself."

After a good shampoo and a plate full of table scraps, the little intruder knew where his security lay, and he followed Mama around every day. He shuffled his useless front paws as best he could while pushing forward with his hind legs, never letting her get too far from sight. At night he was under the covers beside her, so happy and secure that he even snored. Preacher wasn't too happy about the turn of events, especially the snoring, but in this situation he wasn't about to complain. Intelligent though he was, he couldn't quite understand why Mama had fussed about his snoring all these years but thought it was cute when the dog snored, even if it kept both of them awake. It was about a week later when the family was sitting on the porch, and the "poor little thing," as they had begun to call him, came waddling toward them.

"He just putters along, not getting very far, very fast, but he gets there." Mama mused.

Trying anything to get back in Mama's good graces, Preacher said, "Why don't we call him Putter?"

"Now that's about the smartest thing you have said in over a week," Mama said, nodding. "Putter it will be."

With that, life returned to normal for a while.

CHAPTER 10

THE SILENT STALKER

For about a dozen years the Lambs had attempted in their own way to make the best of and to deal with Sammy's illness. Preacher's Putter outburst in frustration was only the tip of an iceberg that drifted silently below the surfaces of their combined lives.

Sammy, with all of his limitations, knew that he was different and not in step with all the other lives around him. Once when he had a seizure at the local service station, a little boy asked his father, "What's wrong with him?"

The boy's father replied, "Son, Sammy ain't right."

Sammy had heard that before, and in his mind of absolutes for Sammy that kind of response meant that if he was not right, then he was wrong. Wrong from what? He didn't like being wrong because he knew wrong was not right.

Sammy was reminded every day when he looked into the mirror that he looked different, but since no two people look the same, of what importance should it be to anyone? Most of all Sammy was aware of his lack of mental acuity. Mama had attempted to teach him to read, but failed, and if a teacher couldn't teach him, no one could, he reasoned.

Finally, he knew that already there were too many "could nots" in his life. He could not read, write, run, dance, play ball, shoot a gun, hunt with the men, date, marry, have children, hold a job, cook, go to parties, shop, ride a bike or horse, or travel without supervision. The list was only limited by his limited imagination, but every day he was reminded of something anew that would never be possible for him. Futility was not in Sammy's vocabulary, but had he known the word, futility would have described his unspoken state of mind.

Preacher had concluded years before that nothing could be done to change Sammy's fate. As was his nature, Preacher determined to deal with every setback as it arose, appreciate the pleasant surprises if and when they came along, and look on the future just as a word, not a period of time. To look to a promising future almost had to mean that Sammy would be the recipient of a miracle or a breakthrough in medical science. In Preacher's estimation, neither seemed likely.

Whereas he and Mama were generally compatible, their outlooks on Sammy and their collective futures were amazingly different. Mama was the eternal optimist. She not only believed in miracles;, she expected miracles. She read her Bible with hope and expectation daily. She looked for situations similar to theirs with a biblical solution, and there were many illustrations of the impossible becoming possible. Divine healing seemed to be the only likely cure for her son, but she refused to give up searching for any answer. She renewed with determination her search for a school or program geared to older youths with learning issues and physical limitations. She wrote to medical schools in Durham and Chapel Hill. She also contacted the Mayo Clinic for advice. Their programs were among the elite in cutting-edge research. Although each medical center had distinguished physicians and the finest facilities in America, after fifteen months of searching, Mama came up with nothing that might meet their family's needs.

Refusing to surrender in her quest for a cure, she assumed the philosophy that patience would provide a solution. And so she waited, always with expectancy. Junior had gone away to Duke for his freshman year, and his thoughts were focused upon completing his education and marrying Della as soon as possible. Jake was in the first grade, and life with Sammy was the only world he knew. He didn't worry about the future.

Church members were universally sympathetic for the Lambs and on four occasions surprised the family with a "pounding" after Sunday night services, usually during the Christmas season. A pounding was a show of approval and support in which friends and church members brought a pound of something of value as a gift to the minister and his family. Gifts such as a pound of cheese, pork, beef, butter, milk, eggs, sugar, apples, candy, or even home supplies would be presented to the grateful and surprised family.

Unfortunately, Sammy's seizures were now recurring with greater intensity. The failure to diagnose the cause of his problem, and its stealthy pursuit of Sammy's remaining health, cast a shadow on even the happiest of the Lambs' celebrations.

CHAPTER 11

THE SIXTH SENSE

In the following days Putter became a Godsend for the Lamb family. Instead of a frightful skeleton draped in skin, he had been transformed into a warm, soft, fuzzy furball—a comfort dog of sorts. Mama and Sammy had kept him well fed with selected table scraps, and even Preacher got into the act by buying him an occasional meat stick at the service station. One day after completing his sermon preparation, he proclaimed that Putter was "a soothing balm for the weary soul."

Typically, when weather permitted Putter would spend most of his day on the front porch swing. By now he had been awarded his own "porch pillow," and Sammy would either hold him on his lap or would carefully place the little thing on his pillow while Sammy blew the harmonica or scoured the land with his worn but trusted binoculars. Mama had apparently forgotten about the new set of binoculars for Christmas because several years had passed, and Sammy was still using his Hopalong Cassidy set.

Although Putter's mobility was severely curtailed by his injured front legs, and although his eyesight had been weakened by glaucoma, the little dog had enormous value for the family. His remaining senses of hearing and smell were acute, and he rapidly became a guardian-watchdog extraordinaire. Any unidentifiable knock would evoke a guttural growl, and the variations in his voice became their own identifiable language. If the intruding sound continued, he would demonstrate his vocal range with a high-pitched, continuous yip.

Even more miraculous, though, was his sense of smell and his sixth sense of foretelling that accompanied it. The family noticed, to their amazement, that if Putter and Sammy were in the same room, Putter could forecast Sammy's seizures with reliable accuracy. Before any indications of an impending seizure would be apparent to even the closest family members, Putter would prick his ears and lift his nose at Sammy, much like a bird dog on a fixed point. Then would come repetitious whines, which would start low and finish high. In a minute or less a seizure would begin, but with his dog sounding the alarm, Sammy had time to squat or sit, and family members were given time to rush to his aid.

Subsequent visits to his physicians indicated that there was no exact precedent for the dog's uncanny ability. The medical community called the sixth sense totally unexplainable, not unique in medical journals, but never documented as a predictor of seizures. Preacher called the little chihuahua a blessing. Mama chose to classify little Putter and his sixth sense as a miracle.

The Eagle, a community newspaper, heard about Sammy and the miracle dog, as they described him, and carried a half-page story, with photographs in the Wednesday, midweek edition. A member of the church had seen the article, and she framed a copy of the story for display on Sammy's bedroom wall. Mama and Preacher decided that it was of such importance that it should be hung in the living room. Except for his birth announcement, it was the first time that Sammy had seen his name in the newspaper.

CHAPTER 12

THE HUNDREDTH ANNIVERSARY

Bethlehem, Preacher's largest church, which was located across the road from the parsonage, had been planning its centennial celebration for weeks. The church's roots had been traced to 1850, eleven years before the onset of the War Between the States. The church was preparing for a large crowd of members, former members, and community neighbors to be in attendance. After something of a quandary, the members of Belfont AME Church and Jordan River Baptist were invited to join the celebration. An overflow attendance was expected.

Since the sanctuary was not air conditioned, additional floor fans were set throughout strategic sites in the seating area, pulpit, and choir loft. An extra case of funeral home fans was donated by the Carpenter Funeral Home and placed in the pews. A microphone and speaker system were volunteered on loan by the local radio station. The service was to be along traditional lines, with singing, prayer, announcements, and a sermon. Preacher's sermon title was, "In My Father's House Are Many Mansions."

At the close of the service, the youth had prepared a brief reenactment of the original 1850 service. Miss Mamie and several of her friends had made children's clothing, including shoes and hats that were to be representative of the mid-1800s. In fact, the ladies chuckled at just how little the present-day clothing in the 1950s differed from that of their ancestors' Sunday best. Finally, to close the service, a free will offering would be received. Since so many people were to be present, the Finance Committee thought it would be an ideal time to have a collection for one special and greatly needed sanctuary improvement.

About two months earlier, a vicious summer storm had uprooted an oak tree that, in the process of falling, smashed one of the church's twelve stained glass windows. The estimate for restoring the window was nearly $600. The committee concluded that if everyone contributed about dollar or so, the church would be on its way toward funding the repairs.

Following the benediction, the crowd would congregate outside for an extravagant covered dish meal, and at two o'clock that afternoon, the Choirmasters Quartet would lead an old-fashioned gospel singing in the sanctuary. About the only thing that could go wrong was the weather. Or so they thought.

Sunday arrived without a cloud in the sky. Already the prayers for good weather had been answered. Sammy wanted to go to the service, especially the afternoon song service featuring the Choirmasters. He had heard them often on the radio, but he had never seen anyone famous in person. Preacher insisted that Sammy stay home on the porch. As a pastor, he felt the responsibility for coordinating a very busy series of complicated events throughout the day, and he didn't want it distracted by the potential of one of Sammy's seizures. Sammy obediently stayed in the swing on the porch with Putter, his harmonica, and his binoculars. As a result of the two large speakers stationed outside the sanctuary, Sammy was pleased that he could hear the entire service, even Daddy's sermon about many mansions.

Before the service even began, the attendance was becoming immeasurably larger than expected. Preacher hoped for a standing-room-only event, which was estimated to number around 350, but no one really knew how many might be able to squeeze in. Fifteen minutes before church began, the Bethlehem sanctuary had reached capacity. It had never been that full before except possibly the Sunday the "new" sanctuary opened twenty-three years earlier. The original 1850 white siding church had been destroyed by a lightning strike fire and a new church rebuilt on the same site in 1930.

By eleven o'clock on this particular day, the crowd filled the church and the vestibule and spread out onto the lawn. The service, although longer than expected, went without a hitch. Preacher smiled to himself as he watched the ushers exit the building toward the end of the service to receive the free will offering from those standing and sitting outside. He felt certain the gifts would amount to more than expected.

All was not glee in his thoughts. He had noticed during the service that the guests from Belfont AME were those in the corridors, vestibule, or outside the sanctuary. None were in the pews. He had not heard them respond to his message conversationally with "amens" and "Praise you, Jesus" as they did when he was in their church. He remembered how well he had been treated when he spoke at Bishop Hardin's church, and he wanted to be equally gracious. Upon dismissing the congregation with a benediction, he asked his members to extend a warm welcome to all of the guests and allow them to lead the way through the covered dish serving line.

For the most part, the races remained separate while eating. Although Preacher preferred more mingling, he decided that as long as everyone was comfortable, he would enjoy some food, take his briefcase and offering proceeds to the office, and prepare to meet the Choirmasters before the two o'clock service. If time permitted, he would hurriedly count the offering to announce an estimate of the collection proceeds from the morning worship to all those attending the song service.

It wasn't exact, but the total offering was at least $525, mainly in small bills. With a quick smile of satisfaction, Preacher tucked the currency into his briefcase, left the loose change in the offering plates on his desk, locked his briefcase in the closet, pocketed his key, and hurried outside to meet the quartet.

Mama had delivered a rounded plateful of food to Sammy, including his favorite dessert, chocolate cake. Assured that her son was in good stead, she returned to her role of hostessing and greeting for the songfest.

The afternoon crowd fit comfortably into the sanctuary. The music began promptly at two o'clock, and the Choirmasters did not disappoint. They opened with a spiritual, "Swing Low, Sweet Chariot," which seemed to strike a chord with everyone in attendance. The congregation was more integrated than earlier in the day, and Preacher breathed a sigh of relief.

It was Putter who first noticed a figure running from the back of the church through the parking lot toward the woodlands that wrapped around the sides of the church. As Putter pricked his ears and began a low growl, Sammy raised his binoculars to watch carefully the drama unfolding before him. To his surprise, Sammy noticed that the person was carrying a bag. It appeared to be Preacher's briefcase!

Perhaps it was caused by the excitement of the moment, but Putter now sounded another warning. This time it signaled that Sammy was about to have a seizure. Wisely, Sammy squatted, then sat on the floor. The next thing he remembered was almost an hour later when he regained consciousness with Mama and Preacher, and the Choirmasters standing around him.

Mama had been the first to arrive at Sammy's side. Between hymns during the service, she decided to go outside to check on Sammy. If he was still in the swing, he would see her exit the church and wave. At first glance Mama didn't see Sammy in his swing, and it was then that her attention became distracted by Putter's constant yipping. She knew Sammy needed help.

Shortly after the service ended, Preacher excused himself but asked members of the Quartet to come by the parsonage to meet Sammy, or rather for Sammy to meet them. Preacher suspected that Sammy had another seizure, and he knew that nothing would make his son feel better than to meet his musical idols. He was correct.

Although he had never met the Choirmasters, Sammy knew who they were by their stylish suits when they arrived. He had completely regained consciousness but was so overwhelmed by their presence that he didn't know what to say. He just smiled and meekly shook hands.

Before he could really enjoy the moment, Sammy remembered. "Daddy, Daddy. Your briefcase."

"What about it, son? What about my briefcase?"

"Somebody was running with it."

Now alarmed, Preacher said, "When? Where?"

"When they were singing … running toward the woods."

With that Preacher raced to the church. In a few minutes, he returned. Gravely he said, "We need to call the sheriff. The briefcase and all the offering gifts were stolen!"

CHAPTER 13

THE INVESTIGATION

About thirty minutes later, two sheriff's deputies arrived at the parsonage from opposite directions, sirens blaring and red lights blazing. Not far behind them were neighbors and gawkers from around the area following the sheriff's deputies to the source of the problem. Preacher was waiting in the front yard.

"I hear you had a little robbery over at the church today," Officer Blythe began.

"I wouldn't call it little. For our church it was sizable," Preacher corrected.

"About how much was it?" Blythe asked.

"We don't know exactly," Preacher confessed. "We didn't have time to count it all, but I would estimate around $525."

"Well, that might be a bit of a problem since the amount of the theft may determine the severity of the crime. Was a weapon involved?"

"Not to my knowledge," Preacher speculated.

"Now don't take this the wrong way, Preacher Lamb, but exactly where were you at the supposed time of the crime?"

Shocked at the inference that he could have any involvement, the Preacher stuttered, "Why, why, I was in the church with everybody else."

"And where was the money when it was taken?"

"It was in my briefcase, locked in the pastor's study."

"Did anyone see you put it there?"

Becoming slightly agitated at the deputy's line of questioning, Preacher said, "How about us going over and taking a look at my office, and you tell me how I could be inside the church and demolish my office at the same time."

Officer Blythe and his companion agreed to go to the scene of the crime. Preacher's assessment was correct. It was not an inside job. The door to the minister's closet had been forced open, the door frame shattered, sermon notes and loose change were scattered all over the floor. It appeared to be the handiwork of someone who knew where the briefcase had been secured and someone who entered the pastor's study with the sole intent of stealing the briefcase and its contents.

"Reverend Lamb, can you think of anyone who might hold a grudge against you?" Blythe asked.

'Uh, no, right off hand I can't think of anyone, although a few years ago two fellas tried to kidnap my son, Sammy, and one of the men said he would get me back."

"Was the law involved?" Blythe continued.

"Well, we did notify the Sheriff's Office by telephone, but we didn't file a complaint, and as far as I know, the two men were never caught."

Blythe made a few notes and then proceeded with his questioning. "I hear you had a big crowd at the service. Folks from a couple of churches, I suppose."

"Yes, three churches and other guests, to be exact," Preacher explained.

"Anyone from the AME Church?" asked Blythe.

"Yes, at least fifty or more," Preacher answered. "Is there any particular reason you might think it was someone from the AME group?"

"Nothing. Just a thought. Did Blossom Mote attend?"

Preacher knew Blossom. Everybody in the community had heard of him. In three words, he was a young, gentle giant. At six foot nine and probably around three hundred pounds, even he didn't know the limits of his strength. Someone had said that when Horace Keever's wagon filled with a load of unshucked corn broke an axle and fell on Keever's leg, Blossom had squatted with his back to the bed frame and lifted the back end of the wagon completely off the ground while Keever was pulled to safety. At age twenty, Blossom was as strong as an ox.

Preacher also knew that Blossom would occasionally find himself in trouble for stealing. There were never any serious charges mounted against him, only petty theft, especially food items like fruits and vegetables from someone's field or garden. Once he had been caught stealing a package of hot dogs from the local service station. Blossom's standard reply for his mistake with a shrug of his massive shoulders was, "I be sorry, bossman. I be hongry. I be hongry."

No one could argue with that explanation, and Blossom would be forgiven with the admonition to never do it again.

"Yes, he was here, but Blossom is harmless. He wouldn't hurt a fly," Preacher defended.

"Probably not. But would he steal is the question, and after looking at your closet door, I figure someone mighty strong might be responsible. I think I'll go down and look around in the neighborhood," Deputy Blythe concluded.

"The neighborhood" was simply a street name for Gibsonville, where most of the colored families lived.

With the crowd of onlookers growing, Preacher knew that by now news of the theft was spreading by word of mouth around the community. He was sure there was bound to be trouble if Blossom was accused and arrested unjustly. He also knew that the colored families expected that someone in their midst would likely be accused of the crime if only by association even if there was no concrete supporting evidence present. That's just the way the system worked.

He was aware that the tension between the races was at a simmering point, and an active Klan made matters worse. Preacher knew they might even pay a visit to Blossom's house, and if he was falsely accused, an interracial fire would be ignited. He had to distract the deputy's train of thought.

Suddenly, Preacher motioned for the officer to come to his side. He hadn't wanted to bring Sammy into this situation, but if it meant keeping an innocent person from being falsely accused, the Preacher had to take a chance.

Not raising his voice to be overheard, Preacher said softly, "Before you go, Officer Blythe, I think there is something else you need to know." Preacher paused, hoping he would not regret what he was going to say. "Our son, Sammy, saw something that might shed some light on the robbery."

"Why didn't you say so? Where is he?" the deputy asked.

"Sammy is across the road at the parsonage, and you need to understand that he has seizures, sometimes severe episodes. They tend to occur when he gets frightened or nervous. Authority figures, for example, like you in your sheriff's uniform, can trigger a reaction. Sammy's abilities are limited at best, so if you want this to go well, you need to be as nonthreatening as possible. He has already had one severe episode this afternoon. But the boy doesn't know how to lie, and he will tell you the truth as he understands it to be."

"Just what I need on a Sunday afternoon, a robbery but they don't know how much, and a witness who has seizures. Okay, let's go see Sammy."

As Preacher and Deputy Blythe walked together, two unlikely companions on a Sunday afternoon, Preacher was acutely aware of the significance of the next few minutes. If Sammy couldn't give the deputy some vital description of the culprit's appearance that could alter the deputy's suspicion of Blossom, there would no doubt be trouble between the races. Trouble could even start before the end of the day. And if Sammy couldn't ward off another seizure, the officer would most likely grow impatient and leave, ignoring in his judgment an improbable and questionable eyewitness … the only eyewitness. Preacher suddenly realized that he hadn't taken time to ask Sammy if he knew the identity of the person. Perhaps it was Blossom after all.

Officer Blythe took Preacher's admonition seriously and casually sauntered up the front steps to the porch, where Sammy was still seated in the swing, playing his harmonica. Putter growled.

"It's okay, pup," Preacher said. "It's okay."

"You must be Sammy." The officer smiled with his friendliest greeting of the day. "I'm Officer Blythe, and I came by to ask you a few questions, if you don't mind."

"I don't mind," Sammy repeated.

"I guess you have had quite a day today, haven't you, son?"

Sammy nodded.

"And I suppose you know someone robbed the church today, don't you?"

"I know someone took Daddy's briefcase," Sammy corrected. He had not concluded that there was any money in the briefcase, since Daddy always carried his money in his billfold.

"Yes, yes. You are right. Someone took Preacher's briefcase. What else did he do?"

"He ran to over there into the trees," Sammy explained, as his finger pointed toward the woods.

"Did you get a good look at the person?" Officer Blythe calmly inquired.

"Yes, I did," Sammy said. "I got a good look."

"Now think carefully about this, Sammy. It is a pretty long way over to those woods from here on your porch. How can you really have a good look from this porch? It must be forty or fifty yards to those trees."

"I was watching with my binoculars," Sammy said nonchalantly.

Totally caught off guard by Sammy's response, Blythe went straight to the point. "Sammy, do you have any idea who it might have been carrying your father's briefcase?" the officer asked.

"It was Wheezer Gantt," Sammy said matter-of-factly.

Totally surprised by this revelation, Preacher sat down in the swing beside Sammy and patted him on the shoulder.

"This is very important, son, when you say emphatically that you saw Wheezer running away with my briefcase. It would be like saying that he took something that was not his without my permission."

"It was Wheezer. It was eggsjackly Wheezer Gantt who was running and carrying your briefcase."

Preacher looked at Deputy Blythe. "There is your starting point, Officer. I don't think you need to make that trip to the neighborhood tonight."

"Do you have any idea where Wheezer Gantt lives?"

Preacher Lamb shook his head negatively. "He and his father used to live down on Buffalo Creek, but his father sold the land, gave the proceeds to his girlfriend, and died of a liver ailment. The end result was that Wheezer has been left out in the cold, drifting from place to place, and having occasional run-ins with the law. Your guess concerning his whereabouts is as good as mine."

"Well, I'll be on my way for now, but I may be back again. Now you let me know of anything you might have forgotten. It could be important."

As the two officers drove away, Preacher said to his son, "Sammy, you did well today. I am proud of you. You are a fine, fine son."

Sammy smiled. For Sammy it was one of the best days of his life. He had met the Choirmasters, helped the deputy, and made his dad proud all in the same day.

CHAPTER 14

ADJUDICATION

It took almost three weeks to track down Wheezer Gantt. He had been sleeping in an abandoned mica mine shack in Lincoln County, about twelve miles from Bethlehem Church. Investigating officers were told that a waif had been seen wandering in the neighborhood, and he was suspected to have been using the mine cabin. Although it took two weeks to locate Wheezer's hideout, in less than eight hours of surveillance, the seventeen-year-old was spotted approaching the cabin, and he was arrested, offering no resistance. Concealed inside an old pair of work boots was almost $400, mainly in one-dollar bills. There was no sign of Preacher's briefcase or anything that directly connected him to the crime or crime scene with the exception of the money, which Wheezer insisted he had picked up doing odd jobs. Since he was unable to indicate any former employer, the money was deemed to be sufficient evidence to warrant that he be placed in custody, and he was held in a juvenile detention center pending an appearance in juvenile court.

Wheezer's past record of skirmishes with the law did not work in his favor. The Juvenile Court Prosecutor was a stern ex-Marine, Bifford Jacobs, who exhibited little patience or sympathy to Wheezer Gantt's plight. The defendant was ordered to appear before a juvenile judge for resolution. In some respects this decision worked in Wheezer's favor, since his case could have been forwarded to an adult court appearance if he had received prior convictions.

In normal circumstances, Wheezer might also have been remanded to his home setting, pending his adjudicatory hearing, but since there was no home setting, he was retained in the detention center. He was assigned a defense counselor, August Claireborne III, esquire, a recent law school graduate and an up-and-comer, anxious to move on to higher and greater goals than adjudicatory hearings.

The case was rather clean cut. A juvenile with a rather checkered past had been apprehended with approximately the amount of money in his possession that had been stolen from a church in a neighborhood where he formerly resided. The defendant claimed he was nowhere near the church, and the money found in the boot had been gained from doing odd jobs, although no employer could be found who would validate his story.

In short, the prosecutor wanted the seventeen-year-old off the streets, and the defense appealed for him to be set free due to lack of evidence concerning his whereabouts at the time of the crime. Defense Attorney August Claireborne III decided not to allow Wheezer to testify in his own behalf since he might incriminate himself and do more harm than good.

A day before the hearing, prosecutor Bifford Jacobs called Reverend and Mrs. Lamb to gain their permission to allow Sammy to testify, if needed.

It had been almost a month since Sammy's last seizure had occurred, and Preacher reluctantly agreed. Mama wondered if the judge would allow her to stand at Sammy's side when and if he testified.

Prosecutor Bifford assured her that the judge would be lenient given Sammy's handicapped nature.

Toward the conclusion of the prosecution's case against Wheezer, Prosecutor Bifford called Sammy to the stand to testify. Sammy balked at being sworn in because he had been taught never to swear. Mama assured him that in this situation swearing was permissible, and Mr. Bifford said, "Could you state your name please?"

"Francis Samuel Lamb, but everyone calls me Sammy."

"Thank you, Sammy. Do you live with Reverend and Mrs. Lamb in the parsonage directly across the road from Bethlehem Methodist Church?"

"Yes, my brother Jake lives there, too. My big brother used to live there, but now he goes to school at Duke."

"Thank you, Sammy. Now on the afternoon of Sunday, June 17, 1951, during the song service at the church that afternoon, where exactly were you?"

"I was on my front porch sitting eggsjackly in the middle of the swing listening to the Choirmasters' music."

"And Sammy, what did you see that caught your attention?"

"I saw someone running across the lawn toward the woods carrying Daddy's briefcase."

"And do you see that person in this courtroom?"

"Yes."

"And can you point directly to him?"

Sammy raised his left hand and pointed directly to Wheezer.

A few of the courtroom guests looked at each other and nodded as if Sammy's testimony was authentic and convincing.

"Thank you, Sammy," Prosecutor Bifford concluded.

The judge asked Attorney Claireborne if he wished to question Sammy, and he immediately went for the kill.

"Now, Mr. Lamb," he began. "Do you ever suffer from seizures?"

Sammy looked at Mama. She nodded. "Yes, sometimes," he said.

"And did you have one on the afternoon of Sunday, June 17, 1951?"

"Yes," Sammy answered.

'Was that seizure before or after the event when you allegedly saw someone running?"

"After, I think."

"Now, don't you think that what you allegedly saw was only a bad dream you had while you were having that seizure?"

"No, I don't," Sammy replied.

"And how can you be so sure of yourself, Mr. Lamb?" Attorney Claireborne III inquired.

"Because I don't ever dream when I have a seizure," Sammy explained.

Wisely deciding to move along to another line of questioning, the attorney said, "I believe I heard you say that you saw someone running while carrying your father's briefcase. Is that correct?"

Sammy nodded affirmatively.

"Well, now, Sammy." The attorney began dropping the Mr. and speaking more authoritatively. "I just happened to go out to where you allegedly saw the person running, and the distance between your porch and where the defendant allegedly ran into the woods minimally must be more than fifty yards, wouldn't you agree?"

"I, I don't know," Sammy said, not knowing exactly what question the attorney had just asked him.

"Well, I know," said Claireborne, III, esquire, "It's a long way, fifty-six yards by my calculation ... and I beg to question, how could you see so well in such detail at that great a distance?"

"I looked through my binoculars," Sammy admitted.

"Oh, oh, yes, your binoculars. What kind and what power are they?"

"They are Hopalong Cassidy binoculars, and they are powerful," Sammy bragged.

Everyone chuckled.

Predicting that Sammy would not have brought the binoculars to the courthouse, the attorney pursued his point. "I suppose you just conveniently left them at home, didn't you, Mr. Lamb, so you wouldn't have to show the court how well you can see with them?"

"They are in the car. I always take them with me."

A bit chagrined, but wanting to drive home a point, the attorney asked for a ten-minute recess, mainly to regain his own composure, but also to allow time to retrieve the binoculars.

When court resumed, Mr. Claireborne said, "With your permission, Mr. Lamb, I would like for us to try a little experiment."

"Objection!" Bifford yelled.

"Overruled," the judge declared.

"Now, Mr. Lamb, if you will look to the back of the courtroom, and you will see some writing, small writing above the doorway. Can you read it to me?"

Since Sammy could barely read only in the best of circumstances, he said, "No."

Again Prosecutor Bifford objected by explaining that Sammy's reading capacity was limited, and for all practical purposes nonexistent.

"Abstained," the judge granted.

"Then do this," Claireborne insisted. "Look through your binoculars toward the top of the doorway and tell me what you see."

Sammy carefully focused his Hopalong Cassidy binoculars and began, "No S-m-o-k-i-n-g in the C-o-u-r-t-r-o-o-m," spelling aloud the words he could not read. There were faint claps of approval. Sammy had at least won over most of those in attendance.

Not to be defeated, Attorney August Claireborne III, esquire, made one last bid before losing total control of the damaging testimony interrogation. "A few moments ago, you told the court that the person that you saw running away from the church that Sunday afternoon, June 17, was my client, Wheezer Gantt, and I am wondering, Mr. Lamb, how you can be so sure of yourself?"

"Because I saw him with my binoculars."

"Yes, yes, your binoculars," Claireborne continued. "Do you know Mr. Gantt well? I mean, have you seen him often?"

"No," Sammy admitted.

"How then could you possibly be so convinced that my client is the person whom you think you saw?"

"He had on the yellow shirt he is wearing today," Sammy explained. "It's the same one."

Completely disgusted with himself for his own lack of preparation, Claireborne concluded. "Well, Sammy, I appreciate your keen gifts of observation, but let's be serious. There are thousands of yellow shirts in the United States of America, some I expect look a great deal like the one he is wearing today." Having a sudden stroke of brilliance, Attorney Claireborne questioned, "Have you ever been to New York City?"

"No, but I like the Yankees," Sammy offered. Even the judge displayed an ever-so-faint smile.

"Just answer the question," the attorney demanded, and then moved into his illustration. "Well, in New York City there are almost eight million people living there, and just for a moment let's pretend … you do like to pretend, don't you?"

Sammy nodded. "Yes."

"Then let's pretend that one day you were walking down the street, a very crowded street in New York City, maybe going to a New York Yankees baseball game. People would be coming and going, first one way and then another, and Sammy, let's pretend that I walked past you, maybe even wearing a yellow shirt." Claireborne moved close to Sammy's face into his personal zone for emphasis. "We looked at each other, maybe just for a moment. Now Sammy, tell me if we saw each other sometime later, maybe four or five months later, listen now and listen carefully, are you sure you would know me again if you saw me?"

"Yes, I would," Sammy said with assurance.

"How could you possibly know?" Claireborne demanded.

"Because your breath smells just like Putter's," Sammy explained.

"Putter's?" he asked.

"Yes, he's my dog," Sammy said proudly.

Everyone in the room laughed, except Sammy and August Claireborne III, esquire.

"Silence in the court," the judge proclaimed, lightly pecking his gavel.

"Any further questions, Counselor?"

"None, Your Honor."

"Then the witness may step down if there are no further questions."

As Sammy and Mama left the stand, the judge motioned for Sammy to approach the bench.

Quite out of character, he said quietly, "Well done, young man."

For most folks, there are a handful of individual lifetime highlights that, upon reflection, stand far and above the rest. For Sammy, his day in the courtroom was perhaps his finest hour.

CHAPTER 15

READING!

Mainly as a result of Sammy's brutally honest and completely believable testimony, Wheezer Gantt was sentenced to serve one year at Jackson Training School in Concord, North Carolina. Although he grimaced at the thought of being committed to a reformatory school for twelve months, at heart Wheezer was somewhat relieved. He knew that at least he could depend on three meals a day and a warm bed in which to sleep. As it was before his sentencing, Wheezer had no idea of where his next meal would come from and no money to purchase one without stealing. Within three hours, he was on a bus en route to Jackson.

Upon returning home, Sammy thought time and again about his day in court. Of particular significance in his mind was his ability to almost read the "No Smoking in the Courtroom" sign.

The Lambs had been invited to Miss Mamie's and her husband, Hoyt's, house for Sunday lunch when Sammy popped the question. "Miss Mamie, could you teach me how to read?"

"Now Sammy, you know we have tried," Mama said.

But before she could finish, Miss Mamie interrupted. "Well, I've been thinking about that very thing. Sammy, yes we can try. We can surely try. Why don't we say that every Wednesday you come up here around, let's say around two o'clock in the afternoon, and we'll get started. Why, I bet that by Christmas you'll be reading up a storm."

"Is it hard, Miss Mamie?"

"Well, sometimes it is, but we will just take it a day at a time. In fact, it just occurred to me how we might get started when you come on Wednesday."

"How, Miss Mamie? How?"

"You just don't worry about how. That's for me to figure out."

Except for several times at Christmas and his birthday, Sammy had never experienced the pleasure of anticipation the way that he felt that night. He was going to school to learn how to read. Miss Mamie nicknamed it, "Home Away from Home Schooling."

Quietly in his mind, Sammy had a vision. He had watched Junior as he packed his blue and white steamer trunk in preparation for his freshman year at Duke, and he had watched Jake with his new book satchel marching proudly off to school each day. More than anything Sammy wanted to go to school. He concluded that going to Miss Mamie's home was to be his starting point for the rest of his life.

Sammy was not going there blindly, however. He was well aware that he was greatly debilitated as a result of his seizures. He was equally aware that his peer age group was coming out of high school instead of beginning the first grade. He wasn't really sure of his limitations or of his potential, but Home Schooling Away from Home at Miss Mamie's was where he was to begin.

Mama and Preacher were aware of the day's importance to Sammy. The memory of his appearance in court was fresh enough on their minds that Sammy at least once had exceeded expectations. Maybe he could do it again.

Mama fixed a platter of pancakes for breakfast, Sammy's favorite. Jake had given up one of his notebooks and several sharpened pencils for his brother's first day. But Preacher, who was never one to excel in giving special occasion gifts, surprised everyone.

As Sammy finished his breakfast, Preacher said, "Son, we all know how important this day is to you and to all of us. When I was your age, I was the first and only one in my family who ever tried to go to college. I felt the exact same anticipation and a bit of uncertainty that you are feeling today.

"Typically, when a person graduates from a school, they have the honor of receiving a class ring." Preacher reached in his pocket and pulled out a shiny gold ring.

"This is my ring from Weaver College. Due to my lack of formal preparation for college, Weaver was the only school I could attend for my first two years. My family didn't have much money to support me, but I studied hard, washed dishes in the cafeteria, and kept the wood furnaces stoked with wood throughout the night in winter just so I could stay in school. In other words, I earned this ring.

"Sammy, I want you to have this ring on loan until you are able to read well enough to read and memorize a passage in the New Testament book of John, chapter fourteen, verses one through four. It is one of my favorite scriptures in the Bible. When you can do that, the ring is yours to keep. For now, wear it every day as a reminder of what you are trying to accomplish. I know you can do it. Here, Sammy."

By the time Preacher had finished, Mama was crying. Preacher had never been so tender with anyone maybe ever, except for the night he proposed to her. To say that this drama was out of character for him was an understatement, so much so because even Preacher had a small tear on his cheek.

Sammy put the ring onto his right-hand middle finger and just looked at it. He had never worn gold. He had never even hoped to wear a class ring. That morning was another life memory for Sammy, and a new bond was formed between Sammy and Preacher that had not been there before.

At two o'clock sharp, Sammy knocked on Miss Mamie's door. "Well, you remembered," she teased. "Let's go to the dining room table. I have a place all set up."

There neatly spread on the table were alphabet blocks, a writing pad, two yellow pencils, and a very big eraser. Two chairs were placed side-by-side, and a small chalkboard, with erasers, stood across the table.

Miss Mamie had no formal education in the field of elementary education, but she had taught Sunday school and Bible school for children for nearly forty years. She loved teaching, and she was able to communicate with children on their individual skills levels. She often thought that she could have been a school teacher because she had a special gift of early childhood communication that few others possessed.

"Sammy," she began, "are you comfortable?"

"Yes," he said meekly, somewhat intimidated by the unexpected classroom atmosphere.

"What would like for us to accomplish with these lessons?"

"I want to learn to read, and maybe go to school, and be normal like other people, Miss Mamie," Sammy said almost pleadingly.

"I know you do, Sammy, but what is the first step we need to take? Why did you come here today?"

"To learn how to read."

"Then that is where we shall begin. When you see your name written on a piece of paper, can you read your name?"

"Yes."

"Can you write your name?"

"I can write Sammy," he said, "but sometimes I can't remember which way to turn the S."

Miss Mamie realized what she had suspected. Her work was going to be cut out for her, and she and her pupil would need to exercise extraordinary patience if they were to become even minimally successful.

And so it began. "Sammy, on the table you will see a selection of wooden alphabet blocks. They each have six sides. On each side there is a letter of the alphabet. Can you find five that spell your name and then arrange them in order so that they spell Sammy?

"I think so," he said. In a minute or two, he smiled and said, "Is that right?"

"Perfect!" she exclaimed. "That, Mr. Sammy, is what reading is. It is arranging letters to spell a word so that you recognize the word and know what it means."

The remainder of day one was spent arranging the letters of the alphabet from A to Z, which was not a simple task for Sammy, but with Miss Mamie's coaching, he managed the task successfully. His homework assignment was to take the blocks home with him and practice the alphabet so that he could arrange the blocks in order when he returned for the next lesson. Next, he was to learn to print his name clearly with a capital S turned in the proper manner. Finally, he was to be able to recite the alphabet from A to Z without missing a letter.

To Sammy, this was beginning to feel like school.

The week passed quickly for Sammy. He worked and studied religiously every day except Sunday, which Preacher said was to be a day of rest. When he returned to his second day of home schooling, he surprised Miss Mamie by completing every assignment without error.

"This week we shall begin by writing the alphabet and learning to actually write three words." Step by step and letter by letter, the boy and his mentor worked their way through the alphabet time and time again, correcting every backward letter and rewriting it ten times to get in the habit of inscribing it correctly. Sammy was tired before the end of the hour.

Since winter was only a few days away, his three words for the day were: Sammy (which he already knew), is, and cold. By the end of the lesson, Sammy could read and write one small sentence, which he was to practice writing and rewriting for his homework assignment.

Sammy was actually learning to read. Better still, Sammy was learning that he could learn how to read.

Lesson three was the beginning of a reading experience that would abide with him for the remainder of his lifetime.

After reviewing his homework, and reciting, then writing his alphabet, and getting his new sentence, "Sammy likes Daddy's ring," Miss Mamie had a surprise for him.

"Sammy, I have been looking for the best possible book for us to use as we learn to start reading, and do you know what it is?"

"The Bible?" he guessed.

Miss Mamie laughed. "That's a bit too advanced for us right now. No, it is a whole book of poems that I have written for you. It is called: 'The Trials and Tribulations of Slim Sam Flim flam'i gen.'"

"Slim Sam? A book of poems for us to read today?"

"Not so fast, young man. This is how we will do it. Over the next few months as we work on the alphabet and spelling, I will read a poem to you, one each day, and all of the poems will be rather short. You can take the poem home with you. Maybe Preacher or your mama or even Jake can help you learn to read it word by word. After you have mastered reading that poem perfectly, we will start a new one until you are able to read the whole book of Slim Sam poems by yourself."

"How many poems are there, Miss Mamie?"

"Probably around ten, maybe more. Are you ready to get started on one today?"

"Yes," Sammy almost yelled in expectation.

Miss Mamie began, "Since cold weather is here, I thought we would begin with this one."

Slim Sam Snowman

When Slim Sam was little, with nowhere to go,
He headed outside to play in the snow.
His friends said, "Sam we think it'd be neat
To cover you with snow from your head to your feet."

Good thought, thought Sam, *for I have seen many*
Snowmen who are fat but none who are skinny.
He looked like a stick, as straight as could be,
And in a moment or two or maybe three

He started to tremble and quiver and shake
His mouth froze shut, not a sound could Sam make. He wanted to
turn his head to say, "No!"
But the kids kept patting him all over with snow.

He tried to walk, and his leg made a jerk,
But try as he could, both legs would not work.
A happy sound was his mother's loud scream.
"Wake up, Slim Sam. You've had a bad dream."

"Miss Mamie! I love that poem. Thank you. I'll learn to read it. I promise I will. I will practice and study and learn those words. You will help me, won't you?"

"Of course I will," she said, giving him a parental hug.

It may have been everyone's unceasing patience or Sammy's desire to learn to read or likely a smidgen of each, but eight weeks later, without assistance, at the church's talent show, Sammy read all four verses of the poem deliberately to an appreciative and understanding audience. Then, putting his poem aside, he recited the first verse from memory. In return, he received a standing ovation.

CHAPTER 16

THE CHRISTMAS TREE

Two weeks earlier, the Christmas of Sammy's twentieth year came and went, but not without tears and emotion. Preparations were in place for everyone to spend Christmas day at Nannie and Papa's farm, as was their family custom, but Jake was recovering from a bout with whooping cough, and Mama thought it best to stay close to home.

That year since Jake was ailing, Preacher and Sammy went for a walk in the woods to select a Christmas tree. In the past, either Junior or Jake had joined Preacher in locating the perfect tree. The family's preference was always a fresh cut cedar. Both Mama and Preacher loved the lasting fragrance of the tree, and the boys liked it because it was always the perfect size and rather simple to decorate.

To make locating the perfect tree easier, throughout the year Preacher would always carry some trimming shears, a pocket full of fertilizer, and some red felt ribbons when he would go on his occasional walks in the woodlands surrounding the parsonage. If he would spot a cedar that seemed to have potential, he would tie a red ribbon conspicuously upon one of the highest branches, trim the shape to a near-perfect triangle, and finally sprinkle a fistful of fertilizer around the base. As the number of pruned and fertilized trees matured through the years, choosing the best tree each Christmas simply became a matter of preference.

Almost no sooner than Preacher and Sammy had left the house and were literally within a few steps from the edge of the woods, Sammy spotted a beautiful, eight-foot, red ribbon–clad cedar. "Daddy, there it is. That is *the* one."

"Now, son, let's be patient. Believe me, there are at least four or five more we can choose from. We have barely gotten started."

"Daddy, that's the one. I just feel it, and I can already see it in the living room with colored lights, and bubble lights, and ornaments, and the star on top, and oh yes, the silver stuff ..."

"Tinsel," Preacher said.

"Yes, tinsel, and presents. It's perfect. Let's get it."

Sammy was so enthusiastic and so excited about finding this particular tree that Preacher couldn't say no. Had it been left up to him, Preacher would have extended the hunt for at least an hour because he loved the process and looked forward to it each year.

"All right, Sammy, this tree it will be. We would have a hard time finding one any more beautiful than this one. Mama won't believe that we selected it so quickly."

So quickly it was. So quickly, in fact, that they had failed to notice a wren's small, perfectly constructed nest tucked securely among the limbs. It was Sammy who saw it first.

"Daddy, look at this! An empty bird's nest."

Preacher knew that nesting season for a wren was in the springtime and that the nest had in all likelihood been vacated for months.

"Well, what do you know? A tree with an ornament already attached. I think this is our tree for sure." A few smooth passes with the hand saw, and the tree fell softly to the ground.

Mama was looking out the window and saw the two sunset silhouettes approaching, carrying the cedar. Preacher had the heavier base in one hand, and Sammy was carrying the lighter end, stumbling occasionally because his eyes were riveted on the nest rather than where he was walking.

"My, my. You fellas came back in a hurry. Did it get too cold for you?" she said teasingly, knowing that Preacher and Sammy, who were alike in some ways, never seemed to feel the cold.

"No, Mama. You won't believe this, but we found a perfect tree, and it has a wren's nest near the top."

"That is a surprise. A tree already decorated. All we need to do is put it in some water and set it in the living room." Sammy looked disappointed. "Come now, Sammy, I'm just teasing. A Christmas tree must have some bright ornaments and some lights, and of course, a star on top."

Relieved, Sammy said, "And tinsel too. Let's put it up."

About that time Jake came weakly walking in to see the new tree and especially the nest. Even on tiptoes he couldn't quite stand tall enough to locate the wren's hideout among the upper branches.

"It's too high," he complained.

"Well, you do have a point there, Jake. Maybe if I am real careful I can slip the nest out without destroying it and relocate it down lower where everyone can see it," Mama suggested.

With hands as gentle as a mother with a newborn baby, Mama eased the nest from its lodging and held it softly in her hands.

"Well, if that doesn't beat all. Would you look at that?" Mama squatted and held the nest so everyone could get a good look.

"Mama, what is that? Is it a gold string?" Sammy questioned.

His curiosity now aroused, Preacher came over for a closer look. "By the time you get to be my age you sometimes begin to think that you have seen everything, but this, dear family, is a first for me. If I didn't know better, I would say that it's a bracelet, a small gold bracelet. See the tiny clasp?"

With the skill of a surgeon, Mama began to work the bracelet free from the intertwined twigs. Slowly, one tiny link at a time, the chain bracelet was extracted with no perceived damage to the nest.

For a moment everyone was silent, too amazed to speak, looking in wonderment at the newfound gift of a gold treasure.

"I think we have just found my topic for my Christmas Sunday sermon," Preacher said. "I shall entitle my message, 'The Unexpected Gift.'"

Christmas Sunday was on December 23, two days before Christmas. As was usual for a Christmas service, the church was filled to near-capacity. Families and extended families were present to hear and sing their favorite Christmas carols and to be inspired with a message of hope and love.

Preacher began by reading the Christmas story from the book of Luke, and he spoke of the humble setting for the Babe's birth. He spoke of how the story of Jesus's coming had been foretold by the prophets, but no one could have imagined the concept of a virgin birth. A manger, a virgin birth, a gift to exceed all gifts. And in Bethlehem. How unlikely.

As the service drew to a close, Preacher stepped from the pulpit and walked slowly down the center aisle. He paused, and then gathering his thoughts, he addressed his congregation.

"Even today, God reaches down to us in the most unlikely and completely unexpected ways," he began. "As many of you know, our family has had a longstanding tradition of selecting our Christmas tree from the woodlands around the church. Some might even think that we put too much effort into the project. But this year, quite unexpectedly, our pattern was changed. Our oldest son had not returned home from his first year at college. Our youngest son, Jake, who had helped me last year was unable to this year due to a bout with whooping cough. So for the very first time, I asked our son Sammy to help me. Sammy himself has some health limitations, but he was more than happy to go.

"Before we had gone five steps into the woods, Sammy stopped me and pointed to a nearby cedar tree that I had already overlooked. 'That's it. That's the tree,' my boy told me. My first impulse was to overrule him, but after all, I thought to myself, it was his first time out with me, and I didn't want to disappoint him. So that was the tree we chose.

"Next, it was Sammy who noticed a small wren's nest tucked almost invisibly among the upper branches. Since the nest was nearly impossible to see at that height, we attempted successfully to relocate the nest to a lower section of the tree so that it could be more easily seen. But the real miracle of the unlikely tree had not yet been revealed to us. For woven intricately among the threads, tiny twigs, straw, and pine needles, made ever so carefully by a mother wren perhaps to resemble a small manger was the surprise that I am about to show you."

Reaching into his pocket, Preacher slowly withdrew his clutched fist. He continued.

"Finally, I have sensed since the moment I saw this treasure that it is not ours to keep, but rather it is today being returned to someone who is here among us. I have nothing but intuition upon which I base my feelings." Slowly opening his fist, clutched tightly between his thumb and forefinger dangled the shiny, delicate, feminine gold bracelet.

Immediately, someone to his right gasped. She grabbed her husband's arm, and together they stared in total disbelief at what they saw.

Vera Cooper stepped closer to Preacher. Her husband, Adkin, followed her. "I would know that bracelet anywhere. It belonged to our daughter, Sarah, before she died," Mrs. Cooper said amid tears, her voice shrinking to almost a whisper. "Adkin and I gave it to her for her sixth birthday, and Sarah wore it only for special occasions. When we found out that it was lost, we always suspected that she had dropped it when she was outside playing here at Bible school that summer at the church, but no one turned it in, and we gave up on ever seeing it again."

By now both Mrs. Cooper and Adkin were overcome with so many emotions of the moment that Preacher dismissed the congregation with a Christmas benediction, "Even today we have witnessed a miracle at Christmas that reminds us of that first Christmas so long ago. Go forth and tell others the good news."

And so in the small country church called Bethlehem, when everyone least expected it, a tiny bird, a handicapped boy, and an act of God reminded the Preacher and his flock about the true meaning of Christmas.

CHAPTER 17

UPS AND DOWNS

To the casual observer, life at the home of Pastor and Mrs. Lamb appeared to be close to normal. Everyone has challenges, a person might have reasoned, and the Lambs were getting by just fine even with a disabled son.

To the contrary, never a day passed without multiple reminders of Sammy's limitations. There were no handicapped public facilities. Convenient parking was rarely available, and ramps with railings did not exist. Bathroom units were not equipped for those individuals with limited mobility, but worst of all, there was very little sensitivity to the presence of sharp corners on furniture and furnishings. The greatest threat was glass, penetrable glass that could be crushed into hundreds of razor-sharp edges by an unintended and misdirected fall.

Even with the blessing of having a little dog like Putter, he, too, was becoming older and did not accompany Sammy and the family in public places. In those situations, Sammy had no early warning system.

Once on a trip to the dentist's office and with no perceived warning, Sammy fell headlong into a bank of holly bushes pricking, gouging, scraping, and piercing his face and neck with dozens of abrasions. Fortunately, he must have intuitively closed his eyes before making contact because at least his eyesight was undamaged.

Hardly a week passed that his body didn't display some form of scar, bruise, or cut from a recent injury. Occasionally around home he would wear one of Junior's old football helmets for protection, but in reality there were no guarantees that he was safe from an unforeseen accident.

Follow-up visits to his doctors were a source of optimism, and sometimes helpful, but only for short-term improvements. The typical diagnosis was to tweak his medications in their dosage amount and/ or frequency, but nothing seemed to provide a permanent solution to the issue of seizures, and nothing stimulated his intellectual capabilities.

In very rare situations there could be a bit of humor if one looked deeply enough. Sammy had been experiencing a series of mild but frequent seizures, and Mama thought it best if he visited his local doctor in nearby Lincolnton at Crowell Hospital.

As he was somewhat prone to do, Preacher was exceeding the speed limit by at least ten miles per hour when he realized he was being followed closely by a patrolman with his red light flashing. Obediently, Preacher pulled over. The officer stepped from his vehicle, carefully adjusted his hat, and walked authoritatively toward Preacher's open window.

Before he even had an opportunity to ask for Preacher's license, Sammy let out a yell from the backseat and began flailing both fisted arms, swaying his head from side to side, and kicking both legs in wild, confusing conflicting directions.

Looking into the backseat, the officer noticed Sammy's situation. "Is he okay?" the patrolman began.

"A seizure. We are on the way to Crowell Hospital," Preacher explained.

"Follow me," the officer volunteered.

Racing in, around, and beside traffic, Preacher and Sammy reached the hospital in record time, fifteen minutes ahead of schedule. To be totally convincing, Preacher went to the Emergency Room entrance, which he had never done before.

"Need help?" the officer inquired.

"No, sir, I think we can take it from here. You have been a big help. Thank you ever so much," Preacher said appreciatively.

The patrolman gave a military-style salute and was off again in the pursuit of justice. Preacher slowly drove around the building, parked, and escorted Sammy into the waiting room, as was his usual practice.

"A bit early today, aren't we?" the receptionist asked.

"Not much traffic to hold us back," Preacher said truthfully with an understated smile.

On the home front, Sammy was practicing his reading assiduously. He wanted to go to school somewhere, and he knew that without being able to read and write, his chances were not good. He also wanted to keep his father's Weaver College ring. Mama realized the task of learning to read and memorize verses in the King James Bible could be a challenge for any young person, and with Preacher's blessings, she rewrote the passage and gave Miss Mamie a copy to make it a part of his assignment. Sammy uneasily resisted the new wording, but Mama and Miss Mamie assured him that Preacher had approved the revised version.

Sammy was to work on learning the verses of the reworded "many mansions" story and one verse of a Slim Sam poem in preparation for each lesson. Little by little, Sammy progressed. Through practice and repetition, repetition and practice, he was achieving his goal … somewhat. It became apparent that Sammy was able to memorize better than he could retain and recall. He would put his forefinger on each word as he went along.

"One day Sam's neighbor old Mr. Cobb," Sammy would read. But later when the word *neighbor* would appear in an unrelated passage, Sammy could not recognize it. It was a difficult problem, perhaps an impossible one to overcome.

So determined was he to earn the gold Weaver College ring that although he appeared to read his Bible verses fluently, he was actually repeating words he had memorized. Whether by reading or by memorization, Sammy victoriously "read" the required Bible verses to Preacher; and in turn, as promised, Preacher officially awarded the ring to Sammy with great pomp and circumstance. Sammy had earned his ring!

Another bright side was that Sammy could catch on to and remember one-syllable words with regularity. Every attempt was made keep each lesson as basic as possible. Also positive was that Sammy loved what he was doing. As pitiful as it sounded, he loved learning, and nothing seemed to discourage him. He continued to look forward to every lesson with as much enthusiasm as his first lesson at Miss Mamie's.

Another ray of promise lay in the fact that some difficult words like Flim flam'igen were no problem for him. It was not rational, but words he liked were recognizable, and those words that elicited no emotion were much more challenging to his retention.

In business terms, the bottom line was that Sammy was reaching his goal of learning to read ever so slowly. The goal of becoming seizure free was more elusive.

CHAPTER 18

FAMILY CHANGES

In the two years that had elapsed since Junior and Della first met, acquaintance became friendship, friendship became love, and love became marriage. After a year at Duke, Junior's life boiled down to one of two choices. Either he had to drop out of school and come home to be nearer Della, or he had to make sure they got married in time to be back in school for the second semester of his sophomore year. The second option had much more appeal to both of them, and a pre-Christmas wedding was planned.

Preacher performed the ceremony, Jake was a ring bearer, and Sammy was an honorary usher. Since Della was their only child, the Gastons made certain the wedding was a beautiful event by all standards, and the wedded couple set off to pursue a new life together, meaning they would be somewhat apart from their families at least for the foreseeable future.

Jake was growing up and developing his own interests. Any sport involving a ball appealed to him, and in the classroom he succeeded as well. He was blessed with friends, and in many ways, his life was becoming his own.

Mama had been appointed to a full-time teaching position at the all-colored John Chavis High School, where she had served on a part-time basis in the past. Public school integration was still ten or more years away in North Carolina, and as far as informal records were kept, Mrs. Lamb was among the first white teachers in the North Carolina public school system history to serve in an all-colored school. Her assignment was teaching English and Bible, five classes per day, five days per week. Her new work left her away from home with fewer hours per week to meet the family's needs.

Preacher stayed busy, as always. He frequently visited his parishioners in their homes throughout the community, and Sammy often rode with him. Infrequently, he would be left at home alone with Putter, but any time Sammy was alone, he was vulnerable.

It was a warm early autumn afternoon. Sammy was sitting on the front steps with his dog. For no apparent reason, Putter walked into the yard, and instead of taking care of his needs, he continued across the lawn and into the road. Alarmed, Sammy had never seen his dog in the road before. Although traffic was minimal where they lived, he knew his dog was in danger, and even more so because instead of crossing the road, the dog began ambling away from the parsonage. Sammy got as close to the road as quickly as he could only to see Putter disappearing over a small rise in the distance.

Sammy yelled, "Putter!" but Putter was gone.

Sammy knew better than to leave home alone, and although his yearning was to try to catch his dog, his instinct was to stay where he was and wait for Mama, Preacher, or Jake to come home.

In those times many women had not learned to drive, and such was the plight with Mama. It had therefore become Preacher's routine to take Mama to school each morning and pick her up after school every day. Jake, also, was attending an elementary school close to the high school where Mama taught, and Preacher would usually get him in the afternoons instead of expecting him to ride the lengthy school bus route home. Jake always enjoyed taking the morning bus ride with his friends, which was agreeable with his parents.

That day right on schedule, Preacher, Mama, and Jake returned home and pulled into the driveway, only to see Sammy huddled in a compact knot in the front yard. He was sobbing.

"Putter is gone," he cried without giving anyone a chance to ask what was wrong.

"Gone where?" Preacher demanded.

Sammy pointed up the road.

"How long ago?" Mama asked.

Telling time was not one of Sammy's strongest areas, but he guessed maybe fifteen minutes.

"I'll be back," Preacher promised, and before anyone could ask to go with him, he was out of the driveway and out of sight.

Two or more hours passed before he returned holding the little, brown, dusty chihuahua in his arms. Mama and both boys had been anxiously sitting on the porch, and although darkness was upon them, they had not left their sentinels, looking with hope for two headlights bringing good news and a safe pet back home.

"He's amazing," Preacher began. "I'm telling you this dog is a Godsend, and before you ask a thousand questions for me to answer, just listen for a moment and allow me to tell my story.

"After I left, I drove slowly toward the crossroads, stopping every little bit to look in all directions and call and whistle as loudly as I could. I wanted to ask if the Turners had seen him, but they weren't at home. Next, was Miss Mamie's house. The front door was open, and the screen door unlatched, but I didn't see her or Hoyt anywhere. I called out but had no response. I assumed that maybe both of them were out in the garden, and just as I started to leave, I thought I heard Putter whining. Suspecting it must be my imagination, I continued toward the car when I distinctly heard it again. This time it was a different bark. It was the yipping noise Putter makes when Sammy is getting sick. I ran around to the backyard, and there was Putter sitting beside Miss Mamie, who was lying in the grass."

"What? Is she okay? What on earth happened?" Mama reeled off in one breath.

Preacher continued. "I went inside her house to use their phone, and the operator to put me directly through to the hospital. They sent out an ambulance, and fortunately they revived her a bit. The doctors think Miss Mamie might have had a sunstroke and are keeping her for observation overnight.

"Without this little dog somehow knowing that something was wrong, the outcome could have been a very different story. Putter, you are amazing," Preacher said.

"He is a living miracle every day before our own very eyes," Mama proclaimed.

"What would we ever do without Putter?" Sammy asked. No one wanted to attempt answering that question.

CHAPTER 19

CHESTNUT GROVE SCHOOL

Preacher and Mama were never prone to having big birthday celebrations. They came from large families where money was scarce, and they were both reared in a philosophy of what was done for one needed to be done for all. Given their family history, individual birthday celebrations for the boys were kept to a minimum.

Since both parents were now working, they were more openly generous. Local shopping was either done at the hardware in Falston, or more frequently they purchased their goods in town at a department store, Western Auto, or the Roses Dime Store. Mama's favorite shopping by far came from either a Sears or a Montgomery Ward mail order shopping catalog.

These two corporate giants competed each year for the devoted Christmas shoppers, and Mama was hooked. Beginning as early as July or August, she and her boys would sit on the couch night by night poring through page after page of Christmas gift ideas. Since both catalogs grouped their gift ideas by categories, the boys preferred the sections dealing with toys or sporting goods, while Mama found jewelry, clothing, and electrical kitchen gadgets more appealing.

Sammy didn't need to look. Year after when they got to the section dealing with radios, he would always point to the table model Zenith, all plastic radio casing that came in either maroon or black. He preferred maroon.

For his birthday Mama decided to surprise him after several years of wishing and patiently waiting, and on February 22, George Washington's birthday, as he would always proclaim, Sammy received his own radio. It was then that he began his near addiction to the radio and later the television.

Sammy rearranged his bedroom so that his bed and his radio could be near his only electrical outlet. Almost every hour there was a program on one of the few local stations that became one of his twenty or so favorites. Although his days were spent in the safety of his seizure-protected bedroom, he became more sedate and lethargic to the point that it became an area of concern for both parents. His binoculars and harmonica sat on the shelf, and more and more hours were spent indoors. He became noticeably pale.

Finally, Preacher had enough. One night he slipped into Sammy's bedroom while Sammy was asleep and removed one of the radio tubes from the inner casing, rendering the radio useless in its altered state. Sammy became convinced that it had burned out due to overuse, and after he had readjusted somewhat to his former lifestyle, Preacher quietly replaced the tube, and the radio returned to normal working order. Sammy assumed that after it had rested it had somehow fixed itself, and he took great care in making certain that in the future his most prized possession was used only a few hours a day.

Sammy's fortuitous decision had its rewards. His renewed interests in reading and writing and his willingness to attempt math at a most basic elementary level, led him to a life-changing development.

Mama announced at dinner one evening that she had located a possible school for Sammy to attend, if admitted. The principal at John Chavis had encouraged her to look into the possibility of Sammy exploring his educational options at Chestnut Grove Preparatory School in the North Carolina mountains near Morganton.

Dr. Benjamin Stamey was the superintendent/principal at the school and was recognized among his peers statewide as an educator of strong character who was able do wonders with atypical students. The school was sponsored by an interdenominational group of churches, but its roots traced back to its Southern Baptist origins.

To be accepted, students had to demonstrate minimal reading and writing skills, be physically capable to participate in routine daily activities, and have financial resources to cover the cost of his room and board, which totaled $250 per semester. There were more than three hundred students enrolled in grades one through twelve, and their background profiles included orphans, mentally and physically challenged teens, and a small sampling of former reformatory students on early release.

An initial trip was planned for the following week merely to ride through the campus unannounced, look at the facilities, perhaps eat a late afternoon meal in the cafeteria, and if possible, peek into one of the dormitory rooms.

Already the family was experiencing mixed emotions at the thought of Sammy leaving home to attend classes almost a hundred miles away when he had never been away from home for more than a night at a time. But in reality, this new option had been the only school ever mentioned with even a remote chance for his enrollment. Sammy was excited about it too. At least he thought he was.

It was a glorious spring morning when the Lamb family left their driveway en route to the Chestnut Grove campus. They anticipated a two- or three-hour drive, and Mama packed her usual travel picnic consisting of sandwiches, several pieces of fried chicken, a bag of potato chips, some fruit, four pieces of cake, and a jug of chilled sweet tea. Along the way they found a roadside picnic table near Bostic with a scenic view of the rising mountains ahead. Mama and Preacher spread the table for an especially delicious meal. Everyone was relaxed. It was almost like a vacation.

The campus was an inviting combination of brick, stone, and frame structures gathered around a spacious 110-acre campus. For the most part each building appeared to be in a state of good repair. The lawns were neatly trimmed, and the gravel walkways were spacious and free from trash. At a glance all signs were leading to an excellent first impression. Mama's primary concern was the distance between many of the buildings. She wondered if Sammy's ambulatory limitations would be a problem. She noticed, however, a student with greater physical limitations than Sammy's being assisted by two other students up a six-step entry to the auditorium. She felt better.

In the background the family could hear a band practicing. They felt almost as if they were at a hometown high school. Seeing several small children milling around on an adjacent playground reminded them that Chestnut Grove welcomed students of all ages. In general, it felt safe, inviting.

No sooner had they parked in a "Reserved for Visitors" area than they were greeted by a congenial staff member who turned out to be Dr. Stamey, the superintendent.

"I'm Benjamin Stamey," he said with a smile. "It appears this may be your first time on campus. Can I assist you in any way?"

Preacher introduced himself and his family, using his Reverend Lamb title to establish instant credibility with the administrator. Preacher briefly explained the purpose of their exploratory visit, described Sammy's limitations, and expressed the family's desire to find a school that could assist him in overcoming his disabilities to the greatest degree possible.

"Sammy, which is more important to you, academic improvement or socialization among peers?" Dr. Stamey asked.

Mama answered for him, "Academics, I suppose. Sammy doesn't meet a stranger, do you, son.?"

He nodded no, although his body language wasn't too convincing in that new and somewhat uncertain environment.

"If you have a few minutes, maybe we could step into my office. We could at least began an application process and see where that leads us," the superintendent urged.

The Lambs were impressed. They never imagined receiving red carpet treatment, but their reception could not have been handled better. Dr. Stamey explained that they by no means were a medical facility, but he had some medical training following graduate school, and the issue of seizures was not an insurmountable obstacle. He pointed out that Sammy's age and almost nonexistent academic background would be challenging, but the school could design an individualized learning experience that would include early childhood instruction as well as some one-on-one teaching and counseling, especially during his initial weeks away from home.

The cost would be $250 per semester. If enrolled, Sammy would need to be back on September 1, with classes beginning on the third. Meals would be provided three times daily, beginning with a short devotional at 7:30 a.m. followed by breakfast in the dining hall. Laundry service could be provided weekly, if desired, for an extra ten-dollar monthly fee. Sammy would be assigned a roommate to be as compatible with him as possible. In fact, Dr. Stamey said he already had someone in mind who might be a perfect fit. All in all the Lambs couldn't have asked for more. What was planned as simply a reconnaissance trip had turned into an admissions interview with the top administrator. Superintendent Stamey promised to be in touch within a week regarding Sammy's admission, and the Lambs left Chestnut Grove with hope and expectancy.

The return trip home was not as pleasant. The family stopped at a small restaurant called Ben's Roadside Cafe for supper. Preacher and Mama were in agreement about how perfect the day had been and how the atmosphere at Chestnut Grove had a soothing, reassuring ambiance about it.

Shortly after all the meals and tableware been delivered, Sammy's facial expression turned to a vacant stare. Mama recognized his situation and moved quickly around the table to his side. He moaned, then at the top of his lungs he yelled guttural expressions of anguish as if demons were at war within him, or maybe even the devil himself had taken control. The reaction in the room was understandably varied.

Some looked in startled horror. The few children cried and screamed. Some patrons ran for the door to avoid whatever was to come. Sammy flailed and tried to stand up. The plates and tableware recently delivered were slung to the floor, spilling and crashing wherever they landed.

One man yelled to anyone who would listen, "Get him out of here!"

A lady said, "Is there anything I can do?"

The owner said, "Let me help you to get him to your car," which was another way of asking them to leave. After the wild animation had subsided, Preacher, Mama, and the owner, with everyone looking on, ushered Sammy outside and into the car.

The remainder of the trip home was spent in deafening silence, with Preacher and Mama processing in their own way all of the events of the day. Meanwhile, Sammy sat quietly in the backseat, gradually returning to civility. Jake, who had seen it all before but never in a restaurant setting, wondered to himself what it meant for the future. When they arrived at home, everyone went on to bed without supper. Although they had not eaten since the picnic, Mama didn't want to cook, and it really didn't matter because no one was hungry.

CHAPTER 20

ACCEPTANCE

Shortly after sunrise, Putter began yipping. Sammy was having another seizure. Mama was immediately at his side, and the episode continued for almost thirty minutes. Preacher partially strapped his son to the bed with a sheet to prevent him from hurling himself from the bed to the floor. Mama placed a wooden spoon over his tongue to prevent him from biting himself or strangling. When Sammy finally became calm, Preacher and Mama just looked sadly at each other. Mama simply asked, "Do you want to make the call, or do you want me to?"

"I'll call Dr. Proctor, and I'll be ready to go whenever he can see us," Preacher volunteered. Although it was a Saturday, Dr. Proctor was available, and in less than an hour the Lambs were on the way to Charlotte.

After a thorough examination, the doctor sat down with the family.

"Given Sammy's predicament, I can't be a hundred percent certain of anything I am about to recommend, but I would like to request that we try a new approach for the next month to see if we can turn this sinister illness in a different direction. I am recommending that we add an extra daily dosage of his phenobarbital but reduce the amount of each dose.

"Also, I have done a great deal of reading concerning various triggering factors that may contribute to causing the seizures. One particular area we can work on is his sugar intake. Some research suggests that processed sugar, if ingested in excess, may act as a stimulant that alters body chemistry, which in turn leads to a convulsion for individuals prone to seizures.

"You watch his diet carefully, especially the excessive sugar levels. However, just as we don't want them too high, we don't want them too low because the body needs sugar to produce glucose. You control his sugar in moderation, and I will adjust his prescription. In a month we will see if there have been any positive results."

Again the Lambs returned home with a thread of hope for Sammy's improvement. Five days later the Lambs received an acceptance letter from Chestnut Grove announcing that Sammy had been admitted for enrollment on a trial basis for one semester. Coupled with that fact that Sammy had not had a convulsion in almost a week, it added up to a good day. The emotional roller coaster ride seemed never to end, and on this day the family welcomed good news.

Springtime gradually became summer. Preacher received word from the Methodist Conference that this year probably would be his final year at Bethlehem Church. Preacher and his family had been at that one Methodist appointment for almost ten years, which was an anomaly by Methodist standards. Typically, a minister would be appointed to a four- or five-year ministry, and then he and his family would be moved on to another church, usually in another community, but not outside of western North Carolina.

The extenuating circumstances in the Lambs' case made a move to another setting difficult. They had grown accustomed to their surroundings. Sammy's physicians were accessible. Mama had a most unique and rewarding teaching position, with her time now shared equally by both local high schools.

Since teaching Bible in the North Carolina public school system was no longer going to be permitted through the use of public funding, seven local churches and one private donor agreed to pay Mrs. Lamb's salary and benefits if the school board would permit it. Their vote was unanimous in favor of her continuing to teach Bible in both schools on a combined full-time basis.

Another consideration was that through the years the pastor's home had been gradually converted into an "accident-proof" environment for Sammy, and not particularly fitted for future ministers and their families. Probably most compelling was the fact that Preacher's parishioners did not want him or his family to leave.

Immediately church committees gathered, and a petition was circulated proposing that the Lambs be appointed to their present ministry for an indefinite number of years. Before summer ended, the request was approved by the bishop for an extension extending for an indefinite period, as requested. By the grace of God, one obstacle had been overcome and a significant cause for concern had vanished.

Step by step, the family began preparing for Sammy's new life as quickly as his admission had been approved. Mama and Preacher contributed $125 each to cover the cost of his first semester tuition, books, and fees and promptly sent his payment to the Chestnut Grove Business Office. A follow-up meeting with his guidance counselor was scheduled for mid-July. Mama purchased an oversize suitcase to begin packing gradually.

One day Preacher asked, "Sammy, what is one thing that you would most of all like to take with you?"

Without hesitation he said, "Putter."

Preacher had thought it would be his binoculars or his harmonica. "But Putter?" It caught him off guard. "Sammy, you know …"

Sammy interrupted, "I want to take Putter. He understands me. He knows when I am getting sick. He keeps me from hurting myself. I need Putter."

For the first time in almost twenty years, Preacher heard Sammy say that he needed something. He had often said that he wanted to be normal. He had wished that he could be like other people. He had said he wanted to do many of the things others did, but never had he said he needed anything.

"As far as I know, pets are not allowed, and you've only been accepted on a provisional basis. Sammy, I don't think—"

"I know what you don't think, but I think they would let me bring him if they knew how much I depend on him. He could help me. Please," Sammy begged.

Being totally practical, Preacher asked, "And who would feed him, and where would he stay? It is bitter cold in those mountains during the winter. He would freeze to death outside."

"He should stay in my room. He is a rescue dog. He has protected me from danger."

Preacher was actually thinking that the family had rescued Putter, but maybe Sammy was right. He had rescued Sammy many times, and they had only rescued Putter once.

"I tell you what I'll do," Preacher promised. "When we go up in July, I will talk to Dr. Stamey about taking Putter on a trial basis, just like you are on a trial arrangement. Maybe they could make an exception."

Including getting paid to pick cotton at Miss Mamie's and testifying in Wheezer's trial, and even including finding the gold bracelet in the Christmas tree, the possibility of being able to take Putter with him to Chestnut Grove Preparatory School was at the top of his list of his happiest thoughts.

Preacher and Mama created a transition plan that might make Sammy's move less dramatic than it was almost certain to be. Twice he had overnight visits at Miss Mamie's, without Putter. His grandparents, Nannie and Papa, agreed to have Sammy three nights at their home, although they admitted they were not comfortable being around him if he had a convulsion. Papa was in his early eighties and was no match for Sammy when a grand mal attack came upon him. Both visits turned out smoothly, with no medical complications.

Since Sammy's meals were to be in the dining hall, the Lambs went out to eat more often, always choosing either an early or late meal, to avoid crowds. Mama ensured that he ate properly throughout the day, with his sugar intake always regulated.

Junior and Della had more available time during the summer and invited Sammy to Durham for a weekend. Sammy had never been so far away without his parents and looked forward to being in an apartment, which would be another first for him. Junior had promised to take Sammy to see the Duke campus and maybe have his picture taken with Dick Groat, the Duke all-American basketball and baseball player who Junior casually knew from having classes together.

The weekend began with a shaky start. "What are some of your favorite things to eat?' Junior asked, totally committed to being a generous host.

"I like chocolate milk in a carton and fried chicken and chocolate pie. I don't like spinach, and liver mush, and sour kraut, and oysters."

Junior smiled as Sammy rambled off his definite likes and dislikes. *He hasn't changed a bit,* he thought. "Well, Sammy, let's take it one step at a time. We have a small grocery store down the street, and I'll run over there and pick up a quart of Biltmore chocolate milk. Then you can have all you want."

When he returned, Sammy opened the carton and began drinking. "How much can I have?" he asked.

"Drink all you want," Junior offered.

"I think I can drink it all," Sammy bragged.

"Make yourself at home," Junior said.

About a half an hour after finishing his entire quart, Sammy developed a blank facial stare. His eyelids drooped but didn't blink. A deep, *"Arrrrgg"* came from his mouth as he dropped to the pine floor, convulsing.

Junior was glad Della was still at work. Sammy's seizures reminded her of her first day on the porch at the Lambs' parsonage when Sammy had gotten sick. Since then, she felt uncomfortable because she was unable to help him.

In thirty minutes or so Sammy was back to normal. The last thing he remembered was drinking his chocolate milk, with no recollection of having had a seizure. From that moment forward, Junior made sure that everything Sammy ate was in moderation. Although he and Della hadn't been informed of Sammy's restricted moderate sugar diet, there were no more diet-induced seizures, and from Sammy's perspective it was the best weekend ever. He was able to see Dick Groat, and another basketball player, Dick Crowder, which thoroughly baptized him into the Duke basketball fan base forever.

CHAPTER 21

FINAL PREPARATIONS

The registration and orientation trip to Chestnut Grove School was productive. Sammy and the family were shown the location of his housing assignment, Greene House, room 104. Greene was reserved exclusively for entering students, and the room was a modest double with bunk beds. Sammy had been given the lower bed for safety reasons. Two small desks, two chairs, and two lamps were the only other furnishings except for two open closet spaces for each occupant.

Although the room was important, Sammy nervously awaited the family meeting with Dr. Stamey. Both Preacher and Mama paid attention to Sammy's every move. Jake and Putter stayed in the car as much as possible. Thus far, no one had seen another pet on campus, and the more they thought about it, the more they feared that their request for Putter to accompany Sammy would be denied.

Unbeknownst to anyone in the family, Preacher had written to Dr. Stamey two weeks earlier informing him of their request for Putter to be allowed to join Sammy when he enrolled. Preacher also enclosed a letter of support from Dr. Crowell, the family physician, whose recommendation might carry more importance than a simple family request. It did.

The meeting had barely begun when Superintendent Stamey turned to Sammy and with a smile said, "Sammy, you will be pleased to know that your father's request for you to bring your dog, Putter, I believe is his name, with you for the opening of school has been approved, and he will be allowed to stay with you as long as he can follow a few rules." Sammy nodded appreciatively, partially in surprise and disbelief.

"Mainly your dog will need to avoid being a disturbance or a distraction to any of our students. Excessive barking at any time cannot be permitted. He must be clean and free from odors. His bodily functions must be out of doors and promptly disposed of so as not to be a nuisance to others. Finally, it would be helpful if he is friendly to those around him. Has he ever bitten anyone?"

"Once," Sammy offered.

"Do you remember why he bit that person?" Stamey asked.

"I was trying to get a brier out of his paw, and when I pulled on it, I must have pulled out some hair, too, and Putter bit me on the finger," Sammy explained.

"What happened next?" the educator asked.

"Putter licked me because he was sorry he hurt me," Sammy said, "and then I licked him back just a little bit because I wanted him to know that I was sorry I hurt him, too," Sammy added.

Stamey laughed. "Well, I can't wait to meet your dog when you bring him up here at the beginning of school."

"He's in the car if you would like to meet him," Sammy said, his personality beginning to sparkle. "He is a chihuahua, and he will really like you."

"By all means, bring him in. I would like to get to know Putter."

In a few minutes Putter, wagging his tail, was licking Administrator Stamey's hand in appreciation for having his back scratched.

"I think we will get along just fine. I never had a dog when I was growing up. My parents always said they were too much trouble. Maybe I will just adopt Putter, if you are willing to share him with me while you are here. Make sure you bring him in to see me when you arrive in September."

"I will," Sammy promised.

Returning home, the family was in high spirits, so much so Preacher steered into Ben's Roadside Cafe for supper. "What on earth do you think you are doing?" Mama asked.

"We didn't pay the last time, and I want to see if they will let us in."

"Bain, you are one of a kind, but sometimes you need to have your head examined," Mama lightheartedly suggested.

The owner stared solemnly in disbelief as the Lamb family entered.

"I'm Reverend Lamb, but most folks call me Preacher, and I have felt badly that I failed to pay you the last time we were here. Do you have enough food for some starving travelers?" Preacher was smooth when he wanted to be.

"Come on in, Preacher, and don't worry about the last time. It gave folks something to talk about. My name's Ben Franklin, just like the famous one. What can I get for you?"

As Mr. Franklin delivered their meal, he asked, "Are you really a preacher?"

"I am," Preacher replied, "and can I ask you a question?"

"I get them all day long. I guess one more won't hurt," said the owner.

"Have you ever been saved?"

"I have," the man declared, smiling from ear to ear, "at the Rock Springs camp meeting back in 1948."

"Praise God," said the preacher. "Could you lead us in a word of prayer before we eat?" With heads bowed, Ben Franklin delivered one of the best blessings Preacher had ever heard.

Sammy, Preacher, and the family never again passed that way at mealtime without stopping. They enjoyed seeing Ben Franklin, and they loved that their meals were always on the house.

SECTION II

LATER LIFE

CHAPTER 22

GOING AWAY

When there is a rite of passage such as a marriage, or a move to a new community, or in this case Sammy's relocation to boarding school, there are mixed emotions. A formal education for Sammy was a lifelong dream come true for Mama, but the thought of him going away broke her heart. Tears would often well at the mere thought of leaving Sammy to fend for himself in a strange new environment.

It had not been as difficult when Junior left for college. He was capable of taking care of himself independently, but Sammy was going to be totally dependent on so many strangers for support just to cope with day-to-day living. She worried about his eating habits, and who would provide him with snacks, who would care for Putter if Sammy got sick and went to the infirmary. She knew he had never handled money before, and although his resources were meager, he was totally vulnerable to anyone's greed. Mama had to force herself to deny negative thinking, but more than once she considered withdrawing him before he enrolled. Ultimately, she remained steadfast in her desire to give him a chance to experience life beyond the confines, and security, of home.

Preacher kept to himself any insecurities that he might have felt, and Jake was almost aloof to the family drama. During the summer vacations, he was immersed in reading and more reading, but always made time to play with his neighborhood friends. He had even begun to think a little bit about girls. As far as he was concerned, Sammy could go to school or stay at home. Both were win-win options.

In his free time Preacher was engaged in a new backyard building project that occupied his thinking and helped shut out the reality of Sammy's imminent move. He was constructing a garage, with assistance from a carpenter, to house his brand new, solid black 1951 Oldsmobile 98.

Preacher was characteristically thrifty and saved rigorously until whatever need or interest which arose could be paid for in cash. In the case of the automobile, he learned that an Olds could be ordered from the factory and picked up in the company's manufacturing headquarters in Lansing, Michigan, thereby saving all shipping and local sales taxes. Southern Railway allowed clergy to travel free of charge once a year to any destination in the United States. The idea of a free trip and no taxes and shipping fees made the transaction irresistible to his way of budget-minded thinking.

Sammy was sitting on the front porch when the new car pulled into the driveway. He loved the thought of the new car's smell and couldn't wait to hear all about the trip.

"Well, son, what do you think about our new car?" Preacher began.

"I wish I could drive it," Sammy said wistfully, forcing Preacher see the car from Sammy's eyes instead of his own.

In a split-second reaction, even Preacher couldn't believe, he said, "Remember, Sammy, how you used to drive with Junior? I think to celebrate my return from a safe trip and your going off to school at Chestnut Grove, I will let you drive around the driveway to the church, into the parking lot, and back home in our brand new ninety-eight Oldsmobile. You sit in the driver's seat and steer, and I will handle the brakes and accelerator."

Sammy yelled in exaltation, "Mama, come quickly. Daddy is going to let me drive the new car!"

"Bain, are you sure?" she asked, already knowing his reply.

Preacher gave her a welcome home hug. "It will be okay. Sammy said he wished he could drive." His eyes riveted on hers. She nodded her approval as he spoke. He said, "Don't you think to celebrate his going to school would be a good reason to let him get his wish to drive?"

Mama understood this was all about Sammy, and if Preacher was willing to risk life and limb and a new car for such an occasion, she would too.

"I think I'll just ride in the backseat," she said with a reluctant smile.

Proudly Sammy sat behind the wheel. He had watched Preacher and Junior start a car hundreds of times, and without instruction, he cranked the car by himself. Slowly Preacher powered the car out of the driveway and over to the churchyard while Sammy steered as if he were the pilot of the Enola Gay war plane. For fifteen or more minutes Sammy drove around the churchyard driveway with a smile of total accomplishment.

When he seemed to be satisfied, he steered the car back to the house and into the driveway. He stopped the motor, removed the keys, and handed them to Preacher.

"Thank you," he said to both parents. "I am so happy that you are my Daddy and Mama. This is one of the best days of my life."

For those brief moments, there were no regrets about the past or apprehension about the future. It was an especially good feeling to live simply in the present.

Two weeks later Preacher was driving, and Sammy, with Putter cradled in his left arm, waved a weak, uncertain good-bye from the Greene House sidewalk as the sleek, black 98 Oldsmobile pulled away from the Chestnut Grove School parking lot. Mama, with her face clasped in her hands, was crying. Jake was staring solemnly out the rear window. Preacher was concentrating as best he could on the street ahead but involuntarily scanned the rearview mirror to catch a glimpse of Sammy, still holding Putter, as they disappeared from sight.

"Bain, should we go back?" Mama almost pleaded. "You know as well as I do that Sammy can't do this alone, even with Putter."

"Have you ever wondered who is more needy, Sammy or Putter?" Jake thought out loud.

Although tempted to turn around, Preacher accelerated ahead. "We made this decision to give the boy a chance at an education a long time ago, and we can't give in to our sentimental wishes now."

"I'm not an overprotective mother, and it's not sentimental wishes I'm crying about. It is exercising sound judgment," Mama argued.

Everyone seemed to understand that life, as they had known it, would never be the same—everyone, including Sammy.

Together on the sidewalk, Sammy and Putter waited, hoping that maybe the family's car would come back into sight. In the past they had rarely left him alone.

"They will probably come back," Sammy silently wished. After enough minutes had passed, Sammy turned and walked slowly to his room. Already he wondered where Mama, and Jake, and Daddy were and what they were doing. His roommate wasn't due to arrive until the next day, so Sammy, holding Putter, just sat on the bed thinking.

A knock on the door broke the silence. "Are you in there Sammy?" rang out Dr. Stamey's familiar voice.

"Yes, sir, I'm here," Sammy answered. "Come in."

"I was wondering," the superintendent began, "if you would like to join Mrs. Stamey and me in the cafeteria for supper. Well, looka there. Do you remember me, Putter? You can come along with us, too. We have a special little room where you can stay while we eat."

Putter licked Dr. Stamey's hand while he talked. It was almost as if Putter remembered the kind administrator from their previous visit.

Although he wasn't especially hungry, Sammy made a grown-up decision and accepted the superintendent's invitation. Sammy's education at Chestnut Grove School had begun.

CHAPTER 23

GETTING ACQUAINTED

Upon entering the cafeteria, Sammy noticed a group of mostly male students sitting directly inside the front door.

"Fellows, this is Sammy, and this is his first day at Chestnut Grove. He and his family live in the Cherryville area. You will probably notice him carrying a little, friendly chihuahua around with him on campus. His dog helps him detect that a seizure may be forthcoming, and it gives him time to sit down, which prevents him from falling."

"What's the dog's name?" one of the boys asked.

"His name is Putter," Dr. Stamey responded.

"Putter, huh," the apparent leader of the group repeated. "A good name, a very good name. Make a note of that will you, Teetime?" he suggested to one of his friends. "Sammy and Putter," he said thoughtfully.

Dr. Stamey smiled as he, Mrs. Stamey, and Sammy approached the serving line. When they were seated, Dr. Stamey led a brief blessing and turned to Sammy.

"Those fellows you just met are all upperclassmen. There has been a longstanding tradition here at Chestnut Grove that upperclassmen select a new nickname for each of our entering male students. The names cannot be off-color or vulgar, but they can represent some visual characteristic of each new boy that makes them easy to identify. That name will stick with them for one year or until they do something extraordinary, which then gives them the option to return to their given name, if they wish. In some schools it would be considered to be an initiation process.

"For example, you heard one of the boys referred to as Teetime. That is his Chestnut Grove nickname. His real name is Albert, and he has been a student here for almost four years. He could have gone back to his original name of Albert, but he's a golfer and likes his nickname, so Teetime continues to be what he is called by his friends. Of course, our faculty refer to all of our students by their family-given names.

"But to continue, in about three days, there will be a listing of names posted in Greene House, where you reside. These are nicknames chosen for you and for every new entering student who resides in Greene. In your case it could be a name like: Room 104—Sammy 'Pup' Lamb."

Sammy smiled. "I've never had any nickname but Sammy," he admitted.

After supper the Stameys wished Sammy well, and he, holding Putter, ambled back to his room. They had made it through day one successfully.

The next morning he and Putter went to breakfast. When he entered the dining hall, he knew he was being watched. Two or three of the boys at the first table whispered a few words, made a few notes, and one said, "Good morning, Sammy. Where's Putter?"

"He stays in the little closet while I eat," Sammy explained.

Sammy chose to sit by himself at a table near the end of the serving line. He had learned over time that the fewer steps he took while carrying a tray of food, the less likely he would be of having an accident.

In a few minutes, a girl sat down directly across from him. "Hi, I'm Callie. What's your name?" the girl said.

"I'm, I'm Sammy," the boy said awkwardly. "Do you go to school here?

"I do," she said. "I used to live at the Methodist Children's Home in Winston Salem, but I have an uncle and aunt who now live about eighty miles from here, and I wanted to live closer to them."

Sammy had never really had a conversation with a girl about his age, and he wasn't sure exactly what to say. To make matters worse, she was pretty, one of the prettiest girls he had ever seen. She had deep blue eyes and the longest curly blond hair of anyone on campus he had seen at least so far.

"Do you like pets?" he mumbled.

"Yes!" she said emphatically. "Didn't I see you carrying around a little puppy?"

"He is little, but he is not a puppy." Sammy loved telling the Putter story and gradually felt more at ease with Callie. Without urging, he continued.

"My little dog showed up on our doorstep one day. My parents said we could keep him because he was so damaged. He was skinny and didn't wear a collar. His front legs were crippled, and he could barely see. My daddy didn't want him inside, but Mama felt sorry for him, and he has slept inside ever since. Sometimes I have seizures, and Putter can usually tell when I am about to be sick. That's why Dr. Stamey said I could bring him to school with me."

"Like Putter, I didn't have any family either," Callie explained. "My mama and daddy were killed in a wreck when I was a baby, and there was no one able to care for me, so I was sent to the children's home literally on their doorstep."

Somehow as a unit Sammy, Callie, and Putter seemed to share a common bond.

"Maybe when we leave I could hold him," Callie offered.

"Putter would like that," Sammy agreed, and for the first time he began to feel more secure and at home at Chestnut Grove.

Later that day Sammy's roommate arrived. His name was Chestley Andersen. His father was a noted political figure from South Carolina politics. Mr. Andersen held a seat in the United States Senate. In one respect Chestley and Sammy complemented each other. He had a brilliant mind and unlimited financial support from home. However, Chestley was mildly autistic. He was obsessive about some things that people would consider to be minor. For example, a speck on his shirt would irritate him until it was removed, and the fact that one of the light bulbs in their room was burned out was in his own words, "unacceptable." He was uncoordinated and clumsy. Shaped something like a bowling pin with a small head and bottom-heavy physique, Chestley was naturally unstable.

Sammy's personality was everything that Chestley's wasn't. Sammy took almost everything in stride. He didn't get upset with himself or others when things didn't work out as planned, and whereas Sammy was typically comfortable among people, Chestley was ill at ease.

Chestley's parents seemed mildly friendly to Sammy but were anxious to return to other matters and were off to Columbia in no more than fifteen minutes after arriving at Chestnut Hills to drop their son off. It was almost as if they were embarrassed to be around Chestley. They barely said good-bye. Sammy felt sorry for his roommate.

"I think they wish I'd never been born," Chestley confided, "but that's okay because that is the last I'll see of them until Christmas break."

Maybe no one is normal, Sammy thought.

For perhaps the first time in his life, Sammy wondered what kind of fairness is there in a world when someone like Chestley with such a brilliant mind could be so neglected by parents who obviously could encourage and support him and his handicap if they chose to.

The following day, classes began. Sammy probably had one of the least-rigorous schedules of anyone at Chestnut Grove. His academic goals were minimal, and expectations were low for any dramatic intellectual development. It was a low-stress experience to say the least. Sammy spent over an hour with his counselor discussing his limitations and expectations. Sammy's expectation was "to be normal." The counselor's expectation was for Sammy to realize that there is no normal, that all people have strengths and weaknesses, and her role was to help him explore his strengths and develop them to the greatest degree possible. For the first time he began to understand why he was at Chestnut Grove.

His language class consisted of his reading aloud what he had learned from Miss Mamie's instruction, mainly Slim Sam stories, which Miss Kiker, his teacher, thought were creative and amusing. Their goal was to develop Sammy's recognition and retention of words through one-on-one reading classes and repetitive spelling.

The rest of his day was spent auditing non-credit courses in geography and beginning math. Both course assignments were to broaden his depth of knowledge based primarily upon classroom exposure with no interactive participation expectations. When he returned to his room before supper a small crowd had gathered in the entryway. They were reading their new nickname designations. Posted was the following listing:

Greene House Nickname Assignments

Room 100: Jerry "Flycatcher" Eaves: Mouth always open
Abe "Jack Rabbit" Clawson: Large ears

Room 101: Quincy "Showboat" Diggs: Flashy dresser
Jack "Crooner" Gibson: Thinks he can sing

Room 102: Randy "Goose" Taylor: Long neck
David "Tinker" Baker: Loves to fix motors

Room 103: Arthur "Scarecrow" Watts: Hair problem
Wilson "Huh?" Roberts: Can't hear

Room 104: Sammy "Fleabag" Lamb: Carries puppy
Chestley "Brainstorm" Andersen: Too smart

Room 105: Andy "Paintpot" Porter: Complexion issues
Summy "Alien" Grier: Big eyes, no skin color

Room 106: Billy "Zipper" Watkins: Thin lips
Francis "Crip" Jackson: Broken leg

Room 107: Victor "Rocket" Jones: Pointed head
Wes "Frogman" Ellis: Deep voice

Room 108: Harold "Hawkbill" Hester: Distinctive Nose
Jeff "High Pants" Monk: No waistline

Room 109: Clyde "Three Toe" Smith: Mowing accident
Doug "Bluejay" Biddle: Cocks head

Room 110: Gene "Whichway" Boggs: Eyes directional issue
Fred "Bobber" Jenkins: Head quivers

In some cases the designations were ruthless, but the name calling was in fun and part of the Chestnut Grove initiation process. Although he did not totally grasp the history or significance of an initiation, Sammy liked it because for once he was one of the guys.

CHAPTER 24

STORM CLOUDS

Mama had given Sammy fourteen stamped postal cards, approximately one for each week until the end of the first semester. She especially wanted to hear from him on a routine basis, even if the card happened to be only one sentence. Not only would she be assured that he was in good health, but she could also monitor his penmanship for indications of improvement throughout the year. Sammy enjoyed writing a brief note to the family weekly, and he was faithful to his commitment. From his short but positive messages, the family began to feel relieved that Sammy was, in fact, doing well in school.

Warm weather was still lingering in September, and the school planned an outing at Lake James Retreat Center near Morganton. Two bus-loads of students were included among the student body on a first-come, first-served basis. Sammy, Callie, and Tinker were on the same bus. Tinker Baker was actually water oriented, and he spent his summer months each year with his parents, who owned a home on the lake.

Upon arrival, Tinker encouraged Sammy and Callie to go for a ride in his parents' powerboat, which they kept moored in a slip near the retreat center. Sammy had never been in a motorboat, and although he couldn't swim and didn't have a life jacket, he was first to get a seat near the front. Altogether six students and a counselor were in the overloaded vessel, which soon was pounding the wake at top speed. There had been no room for Putter, and he waited impatiently onshore for their return with Chestley. Suddenly, without warning, and to avoid a chunk of driftwood, Tinker whipped the craft into a steep left turn. Sammy was totally unprepared, and the motion flipped him overboard. It was Callie who screamed first. Tinker immediately cut the vessel's engine, banked sharply to the approximate location where Sammy entered the lake, and quickly scanned the surface.

No one in the boat wore a life preserver, but without hesitation, Tinker abandoned his drifting boat and plunged into the water. He assumed the worst, the almost certain likelihood that Sammy couldn't swim, and with lake depths of one hundred feet or more in that area, he knew Sammy would be gone in an instant without a miracle. The boy prayed that somehow Sammy would float to the surface for just a moment, and someone would surely spot him bobbing up near the boat. But Tinker knew intuitively to dive deeper.

At what he estimated to be around twenty-five feet, he first spotted Sammy's wildly flailing arm. With a tug that almost ripped Sammy's arm from its socket and several powerful scissor kicks, the two boys surfaced, with Tinker gasping for air. The already shaken passengers tugged Sammy into the boat, and Counselor Dickens immediately began performing a modified artificial respiration technique in the bobbing boat's hull. Finally, after what seemed like forever, Sammy belched a chest full of lake water and inhaled a deep gulp of air. His life had miraculously been spared.

The bedraggled boatload of terrified and thankful students came ashore, and onlookers assisted Sammy to the retreat center headquarters. For the remainder of the afternoon, most of the students were content to stay onshore, but a few of the swimmers enjoyed the beach area, as if nothing had happened. Sammy was noticeably shaken by the incident and vowed never to ride in a boat again.

For more than an hour, Chestley repeated, "Sammy fell in the water and almost drowned," until some of the students finally convinced him that Sammy was safe and did not get hurt. Putter whined and licked Sammy unceasingly. Upon their return to campus, Dr. Stamey held a spontaneous prayer service of thanksgiving for the protection of his students.

In addition, Dr. Stamey placed a long-distance telephone call to the Lamb family, assuring them that a tragedy had been averted, and in an unprecedented act of kindness, he allowed Sammy to visit with both his parents on the telephone until they were assured that he was safe.

At dinner that evening the upperclassmen retired the Tinker nickname, and his former name of David was restored in recognition of his extraordinary response in the face of danger. Sammy's nickname of Fleabag, which had already begun to catch on, was forsaken, and he again became known by most of the student body as Sammy. For a few in Greene Hall the name Fleabag lingered, which didn't bother Sammy at all.

The next day Sammy had a frightening seizure in his room after breakfast. His roommate, Chestley, and several classmates took turns staying with him until Sammy's consciousness returned. Lunch and dinner were brought to his bedside. The school was taking extraordinary measures to provide for Sammy's well-being.

Two weeks later, an electrical short circuit in Taylor House, a girls' dorm, set the building afire, and it was completely destroyed. Fortunately, everyone was evacuated, and the fire was prevented from spreading to other buildings, but like a trail of tumbling dominoes, the disturbing news of life at Chestnut Grove School was beginning to make students and their families uncomfortably nervous.

The final calamity caught the campus totally off guard. In late October Dr. Stamey was traveling to Asheville to speak at a superintendents' conference when his automobile blew a front tire and veered suddenly off a steep embankment, tumbling end over end nearly eighty feet down the mountainside before slamming into a granite boulder. Ten hours later he died in emergency surgery.

The following weekend Sammy, Preacher, Mama, Jake, and Putter returned home. Sammy had been withdrawn from Chestnut Grove Preparatory School by his parents. The move was sudden and decisive. There wasn't sufficient time for appropriate good-byes. Dozens of other classmates were being withdrawn by their parents as well.

The once-peaceful and stable educational community was experiencing a chaotic mass exodus. Classes, student life activities, ball games, even ball teams, and many school events were being terminated, canceled, or postponed until a new administrative leadership team could be established.

Callie and Chestley, Sammy's two best friends, were left with a remnant of remaining students to fend for themselves with limited support or supervision. Chestley's parents were in Washington, and if they heard of the Chestnut Grove trauma, they never came to see if their son needed help or assurance. Callie had no committed family members, and at that moment in time, Chestley and Callie's worlds had collapsed before their eyes.

In time only a handful of the devoted faculty and staff members remained who were available to care for the remaining students and assure their well-being. In less than three months, Sammy's new environment and his opportunity for a formal education, which once had been so promising, abruptly ended.

CHAPTER 25

HOME AGAIN

It took Sammy more than a week to regain his composure. He was lethargic, had little or no appetite, and didn't have an interest in allowing anyone into his life, except Putter, who loyally stayed at his side day and night. Although home brought him love and security, he missed his friends. He missed his freedom. He missed his chance to get an authentic education.

Having become more introspective at school, he wondered *why* concerning the events of the last eight weeks. It wasn't particularly that he was engaged in his own self-pity, but he was concerned about Callie, Chestley, Dr. Stamey's family, the devoted school employees, the upperclassmen who sat by the door, and even the destiny of the school itself.

With a minimal appetite, Sammy's sugar intake became out of balance, and his mild and major seizures returned. His grand mal seizures revealed another side of Sammy that had never before been present prior to attending Chestnut Grove. Expletives poured from his mouth as if he were cursing the illness that enslaved him.

Mama and Preacher were aghast. They wanted to erase those memories from his subconscious personality.

"Sammy, stop talking like that!" they would plead to no avail as he cursed loud and long. When the episodes ended, Sammy had no recollection of his language outbursts.

To reestablish a more balanced diet and regulate Sammy's glucose intake, Mama's short-term solution was irresistible food. She baked his favorite chocolate pie, usually a rarity in the Lamb household, which he alone consumed in less than two days. There was an immediate reduction in the frequency of his convulsions. Two weeks passed on the adjusted sugar intake, and with assistance from his medications and a stabilized diet, the seizures gradually subsided.

Sammy's biggest boost came one day when his mother announced,

"Sammy, there is a letter here with your name on it."

The mailbox stood directly in front of the parsonage beside the infrequently traveled country road. For years Sammy watched as the mailman delivered letter after letter, but rarely was their anything for him. To the best of his knowledge he had never received any mail at home except birthday cards, and even at school his only mail was from Mama, Preacher, Junior, or Della. He couldn't begin to imagine who would be writing him.

It was a short letter from Callie. Sammy listened intently as Mama read:

> Dear Sammy, I hope you are okay. Chestley and I
> miss you and especially our daily meals together in
> the cafeteria. How is Putter? Life is difficult here.
> Since there was no room for me to move in with

my aunt and uncle, next month I will be moving to Nazareth Children's Home in Rockwell, North Carolina. If that is somewhere near you, maybe we can visit sometime. Enclosed is a school photograph to help you remember me.

Sincerely,
Callie T

PS: Chestley is moving back to Columbia for now, and he said to tell you hello.

Tears of sadness and joy gathered in Sammy's eyes. He missed Callie, and he was so happy she remembered him. He put the photograph and letter in his treasure box that Mama had given him for Christmas when he was nine years old—the chest with the lock and key. Almost immediately his perspective on life changed for the better.

Partially to redirect Sammy's lingering memories, Mama and Preacher began discussing their need to build a house for their retirement, which would be located on Mama's family's farm near Concord, North Carolina. Sammy liked the idea. He wanted to be close to his grandparents, especially on Christmas day. Recently, they had missed the big event due to church services, and the idea of living close to his grandparents was a welcome thought to imagine.

As soon as spring arrived, construction began. It was to be a red brick house with white oak floors, a basement, attic, central heat and partial air conditioning, two bathrooms, three bedrooms, a large living room with fireplace, a family room, an eat-in kitchen, and a big porch. Best of all, Sammy could pick his own bedroom.

Preacher and Jake assisted the builders as their errand runners. Sammy visited with his grandparents while the men worked. In five months the house was completed and ready for their retirement, which was still some years away.

Mama also had big news. She had been selected to serve as a delegate at an international Bible conference in Toronto, Canada. No one in the family had ever visited another country in peacetime, and this was truly a once-in-a-lifetime opportunity for the family.

On August 5, Preacher's birthday, the Lambs arrived at Niagara Falls, New York. The family, including Sammy and Putter, ventured cautiously toward the edge of the well-protected and majestic waterfalls of the Niagara River.

As the wind blew unceasingly in their faces, and Niagara's mist spat upon them relentlessly, the family of four Lambs seemed to feel the earth quiver beneath their feet. Like Sir Edmond Hillary's perspective atop Mt. Everest, this wonder was far beyond human proportions.

Since one of Mama's goals was to expand Sammy's mind concerning the enormity of creation, standing at the edge of Niagara achieved its purpose. With the family looking in awe at the spectacular, unrelenting power before them, Preacher marveled aloud so anyone could hear him, "If we can see something like this on earth, I cannot begin to imagine what heaven will be like."

Maybe I will be normal in heaven, thought Sammy.

The trip into Toronto seemed all too short, and soon they were returning to the states and a surprise when they arrived at home.

In the mailbox was a letter from the new bishop informing Preacher that due to the death of one of the ministers in the conference, Preacher was being appointed to serve New Hope Methodist in Old

Town, just outside of Winston Salem. The new pastorate was to be filled in three weeks.

The family was stunned. Hadn't they just gone through this dilemma once before? Wasn't this settled by the petition and the bishop's promise? Wasn't Mama's employment a priority? Weren't Jake's school setting and Sammy's doctors worth something?

But this was a new bishop and a different day. After exhausting every conceivable option before them, Preacher, Mama, Jake, and Sammy began the packing process. The move was inevitable. Church members offered to help with loading the trucks, which they had also provided to assist the family with moving expenses.

When Mama arrived at their Bethlehem parsonage near Cherryville almost a dozen years earlier, she cried when she first saw it. The house was of wood frame construction, small, and only modestly maintained or furnished. A wood cooking stove was the centerpiece in an otherwise stark kitchen. Mama should have cried. After all, the Lambs had left their own more comfortable all-electric brick home before being appointed to the Bethlehem Church.

But now they were again moving into a comfortable brick parsonage that was attractive, in a fine neighborhood, well appointed, and near the city. Yet, this time she cried even harder as they left the little white country home that held so many memories. Even in church ministry, life just didn't seem fair. As the family rode to Winston Salem, she realized again that no one was ever promised, nor should they expect, fairness in life on earth.

Mama was already under contract to serve in the Gaston County School System for the upcoming year, and before they left the county, Mama located a small apartment that she, along with Jake, would begin renting in town beginning in September. Since she didn't drive, transportation to and from her high schools and Jake's elementary school would, in all likelihood, be problematic. At best, the year ahead with dual households and separate lifestyles would be a challenge.

Preacher's appointment in Old Town only lasted two years. During that time the summers and weekends were usually spent with the family reunited. At the beginning of each school year with dual households, Sammy and Preacher became more dependent on each other for fellowship, and Mama and Jake were almost constant companions in after-school hours.

Junior had completed his degree at Duke, and shortly thereafter in the midst of the Korean War, he enlisted in the US Air Force. His first two years were spent at an air force base in Reno, Nevada, with Della and their newborn daughter. The Lambs' original family of five was becoming involuntarily scattered.

Preacher and Mama were good travelers, and if circumstances would have been different, their interests would have taken them to the four corners of the earth. Twice, Preacher was given the opportunity to preach in Cuba before the communist takeover. Each time he readily accepted the one-month assignment. Mama attended professional conferences as a speaker or attendee, and for pleasure she conducted extensive research on gold discovery in Cabarrus County, North Carolina, which was very near her place of birth.

Mama's passion without question was studying her Bibles. Every page of every Bible in her library contained underlined and highlighted verses. Page margins were filled with notations and insights regarding the scriptures with present life illustrations. She was extended Bible teaching invitations at schools and churches throughout North and South Carolina. Although she was limited by her inability to drive,

Mama's speaking invitations often included transportation and occasionally an honorarium.

Together for business and pleasure and to expand Sammy's mind, Preacher, Mama, Sammy, and Jake visited the Outer Banks of North Carolina, Maryland's Eastern Shore, Florida's and Virginia's historic Revolutionary and Civil War sites, and Pennsylvania's Amish Country. One day Preacher asked Mama if she and the boys might enjoy visiting Junior, Della, and their new granddaughter in Reno.

"Wouldn't it be too much for Sammy?" she asked.

"Mama, there is so much for all of us to see and learn traveling across this country. We've waited a lifetime to see the United States. I think we should go," Preacher bargained.

In their new black-and-white 1955 Oldsmobile that Preacher had purchased from the factory in Lansing, Michigan, earlier that year, the Lambs set out in midsummer with no air conditioning on a 6,600-mile round trip to Nevada and eventually into the Pacific coast regions of central California.

Preacher had bought everyone in the family a long bill-riding cap to shield their eyes from the summer glare. Mama had never worn a cap, nor would she, and hers was "accidentally" left at home. Jake much preferred the more stylish baseball cap look, and since he had one with the Duke insignia on it, he was totally satisfied with what he had. From the moment he saw it, Sammy loved his new red-and-white cap. Although he looked understandably similar to a woodpecker, he and Preacher were a matched pair and easily recognizable everywhere they went.

If anyone could be classified as a good traveler, it was Sammy. He commented on virtually every change in scenery, never complained of weariness, infrequently needed a bathroom stop, and played his harmonica more than was necessary.

Jake, to pass the time, picked on Sammy relentlessly.

"Sammy," he would begin, "if you were going to a dance, and you could go with someone who was short and possibly a bit overweight, or if you could go with Callie, which one would you take?"

"Awww, you know which one. I'd take Callie even if I didn't know how to dance," he would announce, knowing but not caring that Jake was just trying to get a reaction.

"Well then, if the dance was going to be at the president of the United States house, and the president happened to be a Republican, would you still want to go?"

Wagging his head back and forth like a dog shaking off fleas, he would say, "No!" with emphasis loud enough to be heard in the next car over.

"Okay, okay, then let's assume that the president happened to be a Democrat, maybe let's say like Harry Truman, but the dance was going to be in Russia, and you could take Callie ... then would you go?"

"No, no, no, no, no, no," he would say until Preacher would interrupt and warn the boys to settle down. Even then for emphasis Sammy would mimic a big, "*Nooo.*"

Obviously, to save money Preacher would get a single motel room for the four of them to share. Occasionally, there would be one double bed and a single bed. Jake could always persuade Sammy to choose the air mattress that Preacher stored in the trunk of the car for any emergency sleeping needs. Each night Jake, bragging on the comfort of sleeping on an air mattress, and appearing to be helpful, would inflate the mattress for Sammy, knowing full well that the mattress had a subtle leak, and that by morning Sammy would probably be sleeping on the unrelenting, hard floor. Sammy always accepted and never once complained of a bad night's sleep.

For Christmas two years earlier, Aunt Dovie had given Sammy a Kodak Brownie box camera, which he carried with him on every trip. Since he was prone to overusing the camera, especially if Putter was present, Preacher would usually not put in any film until the family reached its ultimate destination. When Sammy would tire of playing his harmonica, he would begin snapping photographs with his empty camera. And so, the boys entertained themselves and each other while the west-bound miles slipped away. For the most part Putter just slept, completely content at being with the whole family night and day.

On a trip of that duration, even Preacher and Mama occasionally got into the bantering act. After hearing her husband complaining constantly about slow traffic in the major cities and repetitiously wondering why, with all the money in the US Treasury, the government couldn't at least build a few by-passes around those cities, Mama got tired of hearing Preacher's complaints.

"Bain, you wanted to go on this trip, and you have waited almost sixty years to drive across the country. Why are you in such a hurry?"

Preacher shot back, "If you could drive and had to drive in two-lane traffic, which is usually slow to begin with, then you would understand why big city traffic drives me crazy when I am trying to get somewhere."

"What is our next big city?" Mama inquired.

"St, Louis, Missouri," Preacher replied.

"Do you think you are a good enough driver to make it through St. Louis without coming to a complete stop?" Mama taunted.

Preacher's driving skills had never been doubted by anyone, and he was surprised by her question. "No one can do that with all the stoplights and busy rush hour traffic."

"Hmmm. When you were younger, you probably could," she jabbed.

Preacher looked at her in disbelief. "What are you talking about?" he said.

"Nothing," she said softly.

By now the boys in the backseat were fully engaged in their parents' conversation. They had never heard them pick like this before.

As they approached the city, Preacher tugged downward on the brim of his long bill cap and grabbed the steering wheel with both hands and arms in a bear hug-like grip.

I'll show her who can drive a car, he thought to himself.

For the next seventy-five minutes, Preacher negotiated the traffic, stoplights, pedestrians, sightseers, jaywalkers, gawkers, policemen, and slow-moving vehicles like a conductor leads a symphony. He would speed up to pass through a light when needed and slow down to an almost invisible crawl, biding his time for a chance to continue moving forward at a better pace. Agitated motorists blew their horns at him. By the time he left the city limits, Preacher was probably the first driver since the covered wagons passed through to drive from one side of St. Louis to the other without coming to a complete halt. He was sweating. The boys were cheering their father's accomplishment.

With great satisfaction he turned to Mama. "Well, what do you think of that? We didn't stop once!" he said, raising his voice to almost preaching volume.

"It was fun," she said. "Which city comes next?"

"Fun? You sly old fox—you tricked me into that so I wouldn't complain about the traffic."

"Sly, yes. Old, no," Mama said with a smile.

Consistent with his nature, Sammy had his outspoken opinions about the trip. He definitely liked Nashville because it had county music but disliked San Francisco because he didn't like the baseball Giants. They always made him think of Goliath, who was evil. He liked the mountains because he had gone to school in the mountains but disliked the Pacific because the water was rough and cold and once he nearly drowned in Lake James. He liked breakfast at anywhere except Denny's because the only Denny he knew was a bully at Chestnut Grove School and frequently got into trouble with Dr. Stamey. He enjoyed seeing the smaller sports cars that seemed to be going faster than Preacher, but he despised the Volkswagen because it was German, and Adolph Hitler was German. Good or bad, yes or no, up or down. There was never any middle ground for Sammy.

The trip was the highlight of the family's summer travels. For the first time in his life, Sammy experienced: the desert (too hot), the Mississippi River (too hard to pronounce), Carson City (liked the cowboy, Kit Carson), Stead military installation (if he could be normal, he would join the air force like Junior), the Rocky

Mountains (too steep), devil dusters (far away, yes; but up close, no. They made him cough.), and jack rabbits (he liked because they always reminded him of Abe "Jack Rabbit" Clawson, who roomed next to him and Chestley at Chestnut Grove).

Junior and Della had rolled out the red carpet for them. They ate at Seal Rock in San Francisco; stuck their toes in the chilly summer waters at Lake Tahoe; panned for gold near a ghost town; explored Lake Mead and the Hoover Dam; and watched antelope sprint across the desert. Just when the family seemed at home at Junior and Della's, the Lambs found themselves returning to North Carolina.

Before summer ended, the family received notice from the church conference that they had been given a new ministerial appointment. This time it was to pastor Grace Methodist in Gaston County. In some respects it was a welcome change that allowed Mama to continue her career teaching the Bible. The move also enabled the immediate family to be reunited under one roof again.

Although they had not forsaken the possibility that Sammy might be able to attend another school, both Mama and Preacher were in 100 percent agreement that if Sammy were to be enrolled at another school, it would be as a commuter and not a resident. At his age and considering his level of intellectual development, Sammy's days of on-campus residential studies were over.

CHAPTER 26

TRIALS AND EXALTATIONS

One day soon after their move to Grace Church, Putter began making a soft whimper. Automatically, Sammy sat down. Mama watched Sammy intently, but Putter's whimper continued. In a few moments the family realized that it was Putter's own warning system indicating that he had a problem. When Mama attempted to pick him up, he yelped.

"Something is wrong with Putter. I just know it. He hasn't eaten a bite in two days, and I don't think he has drunk any of his water. We need to get him to a vet."

Being new to the community, the Lambs picked the veterinarian, Dr. Compten, whose office appeared to be closest to their home. Any attempts at moving Putter were futile. Anywhere he was touched seemed to hurt him, and no one in the family could bear to hear him in pain.

"I wonder if Dr. Compten would make a home visit?" Mama asked herself and anyone listening.

"Doubtful," Preacher replied, "especially for a new patient, but it never hurts to try."

Thirty minutes later, Dr. Compten arrived.

"He definitely has internal issues, and they are widespread. How old is this dog?"

"I would guess twelve years and probably more," Preacher surmised.

"I would suspect that he has cancer. I can give him something for pain and take him in for tests if you wish … or I could put him down if need be."

"No, never, not Putter. He needs to be with us," Sammy begged.

"We will bring him home, Son, regardless of the outcome," Preacher promised.

Delicately, as if handling fine crystal, Dr. Compten administered an injection, and Preacher and the vet were soon on the way to the clinic.

An hour later Preacher, holding Putter, returned home.

"It's no use," he began, shaking his head. "Putter's cancer is beyond treatment. He won't live much longer, I'm sure."

Everyone wanted to plead, "No, not little Putter!" Instead they looked at each other, speechless.

Preacher, Sammy, Mama, and Jake just stood there and cried. They cried hard, and they couldn't stop.

Putter lay motionless on his bed and watched the family suffer. About an hour later in an act of kindness, Putter shut his eyes, made one deep sigh, and was no more.

The family laid their hands on him, and Preacher prayed a prayer of thanksgiving for the gift of this miracle dog.

"Do you think he will be in heaven?" Sammy asked.

"I do," Preacher replied, "with my whole heart I do. Ten years ago if you would have asked me that question I wouldn't have been able to answer you. But how, oh how, could the God who loves us not receive one of his creations who was as loving and perfect as Putter? Putter is in heaven now. I'm sure of it."

Preacher had a wooden box that was once used for tools, and he carefully wrapped Putter in a flannel baby blanket, placed him inside the box, and closed the lid.

"Does anyone want to go with me?"

"Where, Daddy, where are you taking him?" Sammy was not ready to let him go.

"Son, we have family burial plots for each of us in Concord where we will retire. I can't say why I purchased an extra space, but I knew there might be someone to come our way in life that we would want close to us. That is where we will bury Putter. The plot is actually located next to yours, Sammy."

Without any hesitation and no more discussion, Preacher, Mama, Sammy, and Jake rode the sixty-one miles to bury Putter in the family plot. Without requesting approval to place Putter in the church cemetery, Preacher dug a perfect grave, and each family member laid hands on the box as it slid into the ground. In his final words Preacher said, "No dog could love more or be loved more than you. Thank you, God, for Putter Lamb. He was our everyday miracle."

After the burial service ended, the Lambs, glancing sadly over their collective shoulders, drove away. There was no more they could do and nothing left to say.

That night Mama placed a wide quilted pallet and four pillows on the floor for anyone who might choose to sleep together. Huddled in a heap like refugees, the family went to sleep arm-in-arm, thinking about Putter and how very much they missed him.

It was months before life in the Lamb household returned to anything resembling normal. There was a blanket of sadness that draped over the family, and it reared its head every time someone recalled a special Putter memory or story. It came back every time Sammy had a seizure with no warning. It came when someone would knock on the door, and Putter was not there to bark. It just kept coming back for months in the strangest and oddest ways.

One day Sammy and Preacher were riding down to Concord to do some yard work around their new future home. It was either a lack of concentration or impatience, but when Preacher looked in his rearview mirror, he saw a red flashing light atop of a North Carolina State Trooper's patrol car following right on Preacher's bumper. Glancing at his speedometer, he realized he was driving sixty-eight mph in a fifty-five mph zone.

"In a hurry today, sir?" the officer inquired.

"No, not really," Preacher confessed. "Just absent minded."

"May I see your license and registration?" the officer politely requested.

Leaning over and peering across the seat, the officer asked without an introduction, "And how are you today, Sammy?"

"I'm all right. How are you, Wheezer?"

Preacher's mouth dropped open, and he turned to face the officer in amazement. He looked at Officer Gantt and his patrolman's badge in utter shock. "I can't believe it's you, Officer Gantt. I just cannot believe it is you," Preacher repeated.

"It's understandable that you wouldn't expect to find me standing here in a highway patrol uniform. I became a member of the force two years ago.

Now to take care of business first. You were clocked at sixty-nine mph in a fifty-five mph zone, and that, by highway patrol standards, is a serious infraction. But I am well aware that I would not be standing here right now if it were not for you and Sammy. By the way, Sammy, how is your little dog? Putter, wasn't it?"

"He died not long ago, and we are still sad just thinking about him and missing him," Sammy answered with tears welling in his eyes.

The patrolman nodded in sympathy. "I am sorry to hear that. Let me see now—I think in this case Reverend Lamb we can just overlook the speeding infraction, but with a verbal warning to slow your pace just a bit. The next officer may not be as grateful to you as I am."

"Thank you, sir," Preacher replied, "but might I ask why you feel as if you are grateful to us?"

"It's a long story, but in a way I was glad I got caught stealing church money, which was about as evil a thing as I could think of without actually hurting someone. Being caught and convicted was the beginning of turning my life around. It was not a slap on the wrist as I was accustomed to receiving. It was punishment for doing wrong, and I was sent to the ideal school to get my life turned around when I went to Jackson Training School. In addition, I was provided with three good meals a day, a warm bed to sleep in, and one real opportunity after another to start my life anew. It was because of Sammy and Putter that I got caught. No one else saw me. No one else would have known.

"At Jackson I also met a mentor who helped me get started on the right path once I was released on good behavior. Living with him and his family, I received my high school diploma, completed two years of college, attended the patrol academy, and here I am.

"I must be running along now but with all good wishes to both of you and your family."

"Would you believe that? Now that is a new illustration for my prodigal son sermon. I might just preach it next week. God, you never stop amazing me," Preacher confessed as he pulled cautiously and most deliberately back onto the highway.

Later that year, just before Christmas, Miss Mamie died. She suffered a massive heart attack at home after a busy day at Bethlehem Church preparing for the Christmas pageant. Reverend Lamb was asked to deliver the eulogy.

In closing he said, "Like all of us, Miss Mamie was one-of-a-kind but in a most special, unique, and loving way. Her life was devoted in service to others. This church and this church's family who knew her will always be blessed by her model of Christian living and service to one another."

Sammy sat in the vestibule and listened. He was sad. His small world of support was crumbling around him.

In her after-effects, Miss Mamie had prepared a leather bound collection of all her Slim Sam poems. Attached was her note:

> Dear Sammy,
>
> Thank you for being like a second son to me. These poems were written for you and sometimes about you, and I want you to have them. Keep practicing your reading with your mother, or Jake, or Junior. One day you will be able to read all of them by yourself.
>
> Love to you and your precious family,
> Miss Mamie

The book was added to the drawer that held Sammy's special treasures, like his binoculars, his harmonica, Callie's letter and photograph, the now-worthless key to the Bethlehem parsonage, and Preacher's Duke University class ring, which Sammy hoped to have earned the right to wear someday.

CHAPTER 27

SURPRISES

After four years of military service, Junior, Della, and their three daughters returned to North Carolina. Junior was named editor of a community newspaper in Lincolnton, which held numerous advantages. He, Della, and their young stair-step daughters were able to live close to both of their families. Della's father, James, had been stabling Junior's horse, Daisy, for the past eight years, and now the families could continue to enjoy their love of horses together. Also, in Junior's newspaper role as editor came community opportunities that otherwise might have been missed. One benefit was free tickets.

Over the past four years, Sammy had been introduced to the wonders of television. He was drawn into the World of Disney, western movies, soap operas, the Grand Old Opry, and especially sports programming. He was a Duke basketball fanatic, but the antics and magic of the Harlem Globetrotters appealed to him above all other telecasts.

Actually, he laughed beyond his heart's content, and Mama sometimes worried that entertainment like the Globetrotters was not in Sammy's best interest. She was also protective when it came to westerns. She did not approve of shooting and killing, and when shows like Annie Oakley opened each show with a rifle firing directly at the viewer, Mama would immediately turn the television set off, much to Sammy's dismay.

It is no wonder that Mama particularly was not enthusiastic when Junior invited Sammy and Jake to attend the Globetrotters game, which was scheduled the following week in the new Charlotte Coliseum. Mama feared the crowd would be too imposing, the noise would be too exhilarating, the food would be too threatening to his restricted diet, and worst of all, Sammy, in all the excitement, might succumb to a seizure.

Junior dismissed all of the obstacles with a shrug, and after his continued insistence, the three brothers headed to Charlotte. The coliseum was not full but comfortably crowded. The reserved seats were directly at midcourt about twenty rows up, in other words perfect viewing for a Globetrotters basketball game or any event.

Sammy had never attended a game that even vaguely resembled the atmosphere generated by the Globetrotters. Children and their families were cheering and laughing long before the game began. Sammy sat between Junior and Jake.

With Curly Neal dribbling and Meadowlark Lemon dousing the refs with graffiti, the crowd went wild. It was during one of those magical moments that Sammy had a mild seizure. He flailed around with his arms and yelled a bit just like everyone else in the crowd. No one even imagined that Sammy was in limited medical distress. The seizure passed as suddenly as it came upon him with no one, except his brothers, the wiser.

When they boys returned to the parsonage, Mama anticipated the worst but heard a much better report than she had expected. Sammy was laughing and excited as he tried to explain all that he had heard and seen.

"Thank you, son, for taking your brothers, but especially Sammy, to see the Globetrotters. This is the most I have seen him laugh since before Putter died. It was good for him, and it is a night he will always remember."

Sammy had passed her test, and Mama was right about one thing. Sammy remembered the Globetrotters game for the rest of his life.

She was more willing to approve an invitation when later that year her brother, Charles, asked if Sammy would enjoy going to the Charlotte Motor Speedway to meet the famous race car driver Fireball Roberts. This time with only limited reservations Mama agreed that it would be another good outing for Sammy. Had she known in advance what Charles had planned, she would have definitely refused to let him go.

In those days Fireball Roberts was a General Motors driver, and any friend of General Motors, which manufactured Oldsmobiles, was a friend of Sammy's. Fireball annually asked Charles to assist him with his income taxes, and in return he would always be willing to do a favor for Charlie, as he called him, if at all possible.

Sammy had never been inside an arena nearly as large as the Charlotte Motor Speedway. Once he had visited the Duke football stadium when no one was around, but it could never compare with the massive expanse at the racetrack.

Fireball greeted Charlie and Sammy in the infield and almost immediately asked Sammy if he would like to go for a ride. Charlie had never mentioned the fact that Sammy sometimes had seizures, although at his age Sammy showed obvious signs of being handicapped. Also, Fireball never mentioned to Charlie that to keep

147

the car from flipping in the high banked turns they needed to attain speeds well in excess of a hundred mph.

By the time their experimental 1960 supercharged Pontiac Bonneville #22 rounded the first turn, it was too late for a bystander like Charlie to terminate the ride. It was now just Fireball and Sammy. Charlie probably had never given too much thought to Edward Glenn Roberts' nickname, Fireball. He had earned that calling card by skillful driving at almost blinding speeds ... and Fireball had been involved in some life-threatening crashes.

Charlie had no idea what to expect from Sammy when the car returned to the infield after three trips around the mile-and-a-half oval.

"How was it, Sammy?" Charlie asked reluctantly.

"The best. Daddy would have loved this. Now I can tell him I have been faster in a car than he has, over a hundred twenty mph! The most he has ever been is a hundred mph."

"We might not want to tell your Mother all of that," Charles advised. "She doesn't like fast driving, especially when you are involved."

"I think you are right. Mama is that way, isn't she?"

"She is and always has been. She is a nurturer, and you are mighty fortunate to have her."

Sammy thought for a moment. "Yes I am."

Several months later, the Lambs faced another surprise. It was early in March, and winter had been especially chilling for North Carolina. It was then that the disaster began. In two days a foot of damp snow was lying on top of a one inch base of ice. With the next week and the next and the next came more and more snow with almost no let up in the frigid temperatures.

It was an unprecedented weather event for the state. Some areas had drifts of a hundred inches or more. Thousands of individuals were stranded in their homes or elsewhere. Schools and businesses were locked down, and most couldn't consider reopening until early April. Families stamped HELP or SOS with their feet in the snow for helicopter relief efforts to find them. With once-secure roofs collapsing and trees falling left and right, there were few safe and secure places to be found.

Church services had been canceled indefinitely, but Preacher regularly surveyed the church building and grounds to assure that all was in order. Sammy, who could have been mistaken for an Eskimo, joined Preacher as they trudged through a narrow pathway of sorts to Preacher's church office.

Preacher made a few notes and attempted to place several phone calls to check on his parishioners' well-being while Sammy sat quietly, staring at the framed replica of a Bernhard Plockhorst painting over his dad's shoulder.

The painting was entitled, "The Good Shepherd," and depicted the adult Christ with a lamb nestled in his right arm and held close to his body.

When Preacher had finished, Sammy asked, "Daddy, do you *really* think that Putter is in heaven?"

"I do, Sammy. But why do you ask?"

"It's that painting behind you of Jesus holding the baby lamb. See the Mother sheep looking on, probably wanting to help, but there is nothing she can do. And look at Jesus and the lamb's leg. It looks like the little lamb's leg is hurt, just like Putter's front legs were hurt. If Jesus cared about sheep, you just know he cared about a dog like Putter, don't you?"

Rather than launch into a lecture about the symbolism contained within the parable of the lost sheep, Preacher put his arm around his son and held him tightly. "You miss Putter, don't you, son?"

"Yes, I do," said Sammy, now sniffling and brushing away a rush of tears. "There was just no one like Putter. No one."

"It's all right to cry," Preacher reassured. "Cry all you want."

"Daddy, I'm practically grown up, but I can't stop missing him."

Preacher put his arms around Sammy and held him close for a while. Father and son had forged another new bond in that moment, which Sammy would never forget. That cold, forbidding day. The bitter conditions. A loving dad. The painting. The memory of Putter. His memory of holding Putter and waving good-bye to his family, just as Jesus held the lamb. Those thoughts would forever link Sammy to his dad, to the Plockhorst art, and to his longing to see Putter again.

CHAPTER 28

RETIREMENT

A year after the blizzard of 1960, both Preacher and Mama retired, so to speak. Preacher was often called upon to be a supply pastor, which simply meant that he filled in for ministers who were unexpectedly absent from their pastorates. As a result, he was usually to be found in a pulpit almost every Sunday.

Mama was asked to teach either full-time or as a substitute in the Cabarrus County School system, and it was another five years before she retired completely. Jake had finished college and upon graduation married and moved to Florida for thirteen years before returning to the Carolinas. Junior had been named to a prominent news position at the University of North Carolina. He and Della now had three teenage daughters and were happily settled in their new home.

Sammy lived wherever Preacher and Mama lived, and now for the first time they were in their own permanent home. Sammy had his own personal television, which entertained him throughout the day. The Lambs were excited to have their first private telephone line installed in their home, which meant that the Lambs could make and receive local telephone calls at will. In the past they had been on a party line, which was shared between two or more families. A household could make and receive calls only if the line was not being used and available.

Among the first of Preacher's first improvements was to create a garden, and a garden it was. Possibly resembling the Garden of Eden, it bore not only a bounty of vegetables but also but fruits galore. Preacher had a grape arbor surrounded by peach, apple, and fig trees. He grew strawberries and blueberries. He even cultivated wild, thorny blackberries adjacent to his little Eden, as he called it.

His tomatoes, which were arguably either a fruit or a vegetable, were renowned and plentiful. Each harvesting season he and Sammy would load the car with tomatoes, green beans, and corn, and make rounds throughout the neighborhood sometimes feeding the downtrodden and hungry or taking gifts to local business and community friends who might offer to give Sammy or Preacher a free haircut or car wash in exchange for their garden bounty. It was a symbiotic relationship between Preacher and his sheep, and he enjoyed it.

Time and again Mama would warn, "Bain, it's too hot out there in the garden. You had better come in before you have a sunstroke. Remember Miss Mamie. She was never quite the same after she fainted from overheating."

Preacher could have given Mama the same advice as well. The crops that he harvested came to the house. Corn was shucked and silked; beans were cleaned, strung, and snapped; cucumbers, squash, okra, potatoes, peas, cantaloupes, and watermelons needed to be prepared immediately for future uses. The grapes, muscadines, scuppernongs, and all berries were a mess. Mama made jams and jellies enough to last for an entire year. The Lambs had begun to live a farmer's life and worked like slaves during the summer. Early to bed and early to rise became their routine.

Sammy was a supportive onlooker and helper. He ran a few errands for Preacher and Mama, answered the telephone, and washed and dried dishes daily. The rest of his time was divided between watching television and making his daily telephone calls, "to talk about nothing," as Preacher often referred to it.

On February 22, 1970, Sammy received mail. It was a birthday card written in a familiar writing style but with no return address. It read:

Happy birthday, Sammy,

Hope you are doing well,

Love, Callie T

Sammy was surprised. He had not heard from Callie in years. How did she know where he lived? How did she locate him? And *love*? Callie had never used the word love before.

Mama and Preacher were mildly interested in the mystery but only to ask about the T at the end of her name. "That's a cross," Sammy explained. "Her last name is Cross."

After that, about every two years or so, Sammy would receive either a Christmas card or a birthday card from Callie. Always it would end with Love, Callie T, and always the return address would be missing. The postmark was never from the same location, but it would be from a North or South Carolina town or city. Sammy looked forward each year religiously for his card from Callie, and whenever it arrived, he placed it in his treasure box, the same one that had been with him since childhood.

By 1976 Preacher had slowed down quite a bit. His preaching engagements had become infrequent, but each year he would at least attend the Methodist Church's annual conference, which was held at different sites around the state. Most frequently it met at the Lake Junaluska Retreat Center near Asheville. He loved to hobnob with his colleagues from years past, listen to good sermons, and join in the singing of many of his favorite old standby hymns. It was his connection to a life that he and his family had lived. Once he was called upon by the bishop to lead the congregation in an opening invocation before several thousand attendees. That prayer and his opening comments were one of the many hallmarks of his preaching ministry.

Before he began his prayer, he related to the audience how he, a humble, poor, lowly, unnoticed, and uneducated farm boy from rural North Carolina, had received his call to preach. He was only eleven years old and was picking apples in the family orchard when he felt a piercing beam of light fall directly upon him accompanied by the words, "Follow me, and I shall anoint you to lead others to me." Grandma Lamb had regularly read to the children each night from the Bible, and he knew what his encounter meant. Someway, somehow he would be led to become a minister of the gospel. From that day forward until the drawing of his last breath, Preacher became just that—a preacher.

Mama and Sammy, who now was more capable of functioning in large audiences, beamed with pride. Mama, especially, knew how much this meant to her husband to be recognized by his peers, if only for a passing moment. When he returned to his seat, she gave him a loving smile and held softly to his hand.

Afterward the family had lunch with the bishop and the other program participants. Preacher sat next to his friend and Duke Divinity School roommate, Charlie Goodson. Together for the greater part of the afternoon, they shared a lifetime of memories together about how their life journeys had taken them in such different directions only to arrive at the same point in 1976. Following lunch the old friends, arm in arm, parted again. This time they vowed not to let so many years pass apart from each other.

CHAPTER 29

Mama and Sammy

It had been like so many other summer days. Preacher and Sammy walked to the garden to check the plants and pull a few weeds. This particular garden was not as ambitious as those in earlier years. Preacher had fewer vegetables and fewer expectations than ever before. Mama had convinced him wisely that growing enough to serve family, extended family, friends, neighbors, and strangers was just too much at their ages. Bain was in his mid-eighties, and Mama was several years younger.

"Son, I feel a bit lightheaded today. I don't think we'll be here long," Preacher said as Sammy sat down in the shade to stay cool.

After only ten minutes, Preacher retreated from the garden. "I think I've done enough for today. Let's go to the house."

While he was showering, Mama heard him fall. "Bain," she called, "are you all right?"

There was no response. Mama found him in the shower, breathing but unconscious. An ambulance took him to the nearest hospital, and it was determined that Preacher had suffered a massive stroke. His attending physician, Dr. Young, gave Mama the news.

"His prognosis is very poor, and we don't expect that he will live through the night. If he survives more than seventy-two hours, it will be a miracle, but not a blessing.

"I'm sorry to deliver the test report, but if he lives, which is doubtful, Reverend Lamb will probably be an invalid who needs round-the-clock assistance at best. The stroke did substantial damage. I suggest that you notify all of the immediate family as soon as possible."

Mama was trembling. Sammy had never seen her tremble. She had always been so strong. Tears began to stream down Sammy's face. *Daddy can't hear me, and I'm so sorry that I can't even tell him good-bye,* he thought. *I always expected that I would die first. I am the sick one, the weak one. Without Daddy we don't even have anyone to drive the car.*

Junior was notified in Chapel Hill, and Jake was at a meeting in Georgia when they received the news from Mother's brother, Charles. Both boys were on the way immediately, and by midnight the family stood at Preacher's side.

He was breathing calmly but otherwise lay motionless and unresponsive. By midafternoon the following day, all three sons were exhausted. Mama had been taking a few naps at Preacher's bedside, refusing to leave the room, and she urged the boys to go home for a while. As they entered the front door, the telephone was ringing.

"He's gone to heaven," Mama said in tears. "He passed away calmly about two minutes ago."

The funeral service was packed, as expected, and Sammy sat in the car until the crowd gathered around the grave site. Mama had asked Bishop Hardin to deliver the eulogy, but he was in declining health and could not attend the service. Preacher's schoolmate and friend, Charlie Goodson, agreed to lead the celebration of Preacher Lamb's life. Preacher was laid to rest in a plot near Putter's little grave.

The crowd went home. Junior and Jake lingered at the family's home for two or three days, but both needed to return to their own families and work responsibilities. With uncertainty about Mama and Sammy's futures, they said their good-byes and departed in opposite directions.

Mama and Sammy were left alone.

Surprisingly to some, Mama proved to be much stronger and better prepared than anyone expected. Her first major task was to arrange occasional transportation for herself and Sammy. With some of her brothers and sisters living nearby, the issue of transportation was resolved without difficulty.

Before his death Preacher had officially conferred his Duke class ring to Sammy with no provisions or strings attached. Sammy could wear it whenever, wherever, and however he wanted. Sammy assumed that if it was permissible to wear the Duke ring, then it would go on his middle finger, and the Weaver College ring was moved to his right hand index finger. In those days three rings on any male was a bit over the top, but Sammy wore them all with pride.

For some unknown reason, possibly television and country music influences, Sammy returned to his harmonica with a renewed fervor. He could blow it as long and as loud as he chose, and Mama never discouraged him. If one didn't know better, a person might have perceived Sammy as an off-the-wall entertainer, an eclectic, avant-garde musician perhaps, with his jewelry and somewhat nebulous musical arrangements. Most of all, Sammy was reasonably happy. He and Mama would sit at the kitchen table or outside on the porch and talk for hours, retelling stories that both of them had heard before but enjoying them again just the same.

Mama was a charter member of the local Daughters of the American Revolution chapter, and she invited the group to hold their annual meeting in her home. Assuming Sammy would be watching television, she entertained the ladies at the far end of the home, but as they were about to start, she heard Sammy playing his harmonica. Nonchalantly, she moved close to the door and pushed it shut.

Sammy was obviously in a festive mood, and Mama was just about ready to tell him to wait until later when one of the ladies said, "I love the sound of a harmonica. Is that your son playing?"

Delicately Mama said, "Well, yes it is, but you see Sammy is—"

"Quite talented, no doubt," a lady said, finishing the sentence for Mama.

"Do you think so?" Mama asked, wondering if her guest had spoken out of courtesy.

"Yes, I do. I wish he would come on out here and play something for us to enjoy. I know how you must treasure having him around to play for you throughout the day. Wouldn't the rest of you like to hear him play a selection for us."

"Yes," they agreed in unison.

Mama dubiously asked Sammy to play something for the ladies while she finished arranging the refreshments. Knowing no better and having not a shy bone in his body, Sammy wobbled into the living room, hair askew, wearing three rings, two gold and one silver, and without introduction began to play. It was only when Mama had set out all of the refreshments that she asked him to wrap up his concert.

The ladies clapped and insisted on him being their entertainment if and when they ever returned. Mama never was sure if the ladies actually enjoyed his playing or were just being nice. That evening as he watched television, Sammy thought to himself that finally all his years of practice on the harmonica had paid off. He had actually performed, and the people had enjoyed it.

After the meeting ended and the guests were gone, Mama went to Sammy's room to check on him.

"Sammy, the ladies really seemed to enjoy your harmonica music. Thank you for being our entertainment tonight."

"Mama, I did my best, my dead level best. I wonder if I will ever be able to play before a group like that again."

CHAPTER 30

BEGINNINGS AND ENDINGS

For years Mama had talked about her undergraduate college days at Asbury College in Wilmore, Kentucky. While there she had met Bain, who had transferred to Asbury after graduating from Weaver College.

Those distant days were her first time away from home and a daunting experience to travel almost five hundred miles by bus, alone, on poor roads through the Smoky Mountains to attend a college she had never seen before. While there she and Bain fell in love and planned to marry after graduation. They also had established many lasting friendships with their classmates, and every ten years or so they drove back to Asbury to reconnect with their friends at alumni homecoming reunions.

One of their favorite couples was Harry Wallace and Mildred Blake, both from Florida. After graduation they, too, married and returned to their home state. Harry became a Methodist minister, which was his lifelong calling and desire. Harry was and always had been flamboyant. People just seemed to navigate to him.

One afternoon when Mama was at home and seemed to be missing Bain more than usual, the telephone rang. "Lena, you may remember me, but in case you don't, this is Harry Wallace from our Asbury College years."

Mama almost fainted. "Harry, how are you, where are you, and when might you be coming this way?" she blurted before she could stop herself.

He laughed, and before the conversation ended, they had been on the phone for over four hours. Even Sammy, who was widely known among friends for his endless conversations about nothing, couldn't believe his ears. Mama was prattling along and giggling like a teenager.

"Mama," Sammy scolded. "Who was that? I have never heard you talk that way before."

"Oh, Harry is so much fun, and he always has been. It's been almost ten years since we last chatted, and we had a lot of catching up to do."

With that explanation and for no other logical or conceivable reason, Mama went to her purse, spread on a layer of lipstick, brushed her hair, looked in the mirror once more for good measure, and then went back to the kitchen to continue washing dishes, humming as she worked. At eighty Mama had a special friend.

Their romance, and it was a romance, was short but loving. Harry had lost his wife of over fifty years several years earlier, and at this stage of life Harry and Mama needed each other and wanted to be together as much as possible. Over the next year he traveled to North Carolina twice to see Lena Dear, as he called her, and once she came to Florida "to see her family" and of course, to see Harry while she was there.

One night Harry called Mama, and asked, "How would you and Sammy like to fly to Florida for a week or more, if you can?"

Without considering any limitations or stumbling blocks that could be incurred along the way because of Sammy, Mama said, "We'd love to."

Ten days later Sammy was strapped securely in a window seat beside Mama, and together they were on a Piedmont Airlines jet plane bound for Tampa, Florida. Sammy wasn't sure if he wanted to fly, but if it was anything like riding with Fireball Roberts, he was good to go. It was better. He and Mama, who also had never flown before, were living life to the fullest.

After two weeks of nonstop activities, Sammy, and Mama sporting her first ever suntan, returned to Charlotte. Together with Harry, they had toured Busch Gardens, Bok Tower, and Sea World. They also took a glass-bottom boat ride at Silver Springs. They walked in the sands of St. Petersburg Beach and dined on the water overlooking the Gulf of Mexico. If vacations were listed in rank order, this one was near the top of Mama's list.

Sammy had gotten along better than Mama even hoped he would. When there were activities that appeared to be too demanding for him, one of Harry's neighbors who happened to be a Duke alumnus, would stay with Sammy while Harry and Lena Dear were away.

During their flight back home, Mama composed a letter of appreciation to Harry. She thanked him for giving her a new lease on life and for giving Sammy the time of his life. She told him that nothing could have pleased her more than their visit together.

Because of Harry she could dream again. A short time later Harry was diagnosed with incurable cancer and died shortly thereafter. She never saw him again. Mama, understandably, was devastated.

In retrospect, Mama's decline was the likely result of the combined losses of Bain and Harry, and her sister, Bess, all of whom died within three years of each other, but after losing Harry, Mama was never the same. Her final dream had vanished, and in a short while, she began showing signs of dementia.

The first indication of ensuing problems was a broken hip and subsequent replacement surgery. Sammy couldn't be left at home alone, and the brothers decided that an assisted living facility was his only option, at least for the short term. During rehabilitation Mama was moved to the same facility where Sammy was located, and they were able to see each other daily. Every attempt to steer them back to their home was unsuccessful. With Mama's condition deteriorating, she and Sammy were transferred to a more suitable and comfortable retirement environment.

As time passed, Sammy became more physically unstable and less mobile, which necessitated his use of a walker and sometime later a wheelchair. While Mama slipped away, she gradually lost touch with everything and everyone in the world around her. Rather than live in the isolation of his own world, Sammy began to make the most of his assisted living quarters.

The nurses were kind and attentive to him. Junior, who was now retired and living in the home place, came to see Sammy daily. Jake and his family had moved permanently from Florida back to North Carolina several years earlier. Although he traveled periodically in his work, Jake, his wife, and their two daughters were able to visit Sammy and Mama several times a month, primarily on weekends.

In his waking hours Sammy partially withdrew from television and began roaming the halls in his wheelchair, visiting with anyone who wanted to talk. For the first time in his life, he was more mentally and physically capable than most of the residents around him. People enjoyed hearing him play his harmonica, even if they didn't recognize the tunes, and he became a familiar and welcomed face to all of the residents. Everyone knew Sammy.

Church services were conducted each Sunday in the cafeteria, and Sammy led the singing. Since he was allowed to select the music, he chose all of his favorite gospel hymns. During the Christmas season, in addition to several other carols, he made sure that every Sunday they sang "Silent Night," "Away in a Manger," and "Joy to the World," his three favorites. Occasionally he would play a harmonica solo as the anthem for the service. For the first time in his life at age sixty-five, Sammy was a leader.

Sammy didn't enjoy the repetitious menus, but the staff kept his blood sugar intake monitored with precision, and his convulsions were a rarity. He loved outings, and among staff, family, and friends, he was able to get away from his setting and stay in touch with the world around him. It was on those opportunities that Sammy was able to select his own menu, which either had something to do with hamburgers and a chocolate milkshake or bar-b-que and sweet tea.

Every year Sammy was able to attend family gatherings highlighted by the annual Christmas party at Nannie and Papa's home, which had been a tradition for as long as he could remember. The fact that there were thirteen steps to the main level of the farmhouse, and the fact that he was in a wheelchair, never posed a problem. There was no shortage of hearty males to assist him, and conquering the steps was never an obstacle.

Periodically throughout the year, Sammy was treated by a family member to an evening at the drive-in theater. It reminded him of the many outings with Mama and Preacher, who seemed to enjoy an outdoor movie theater as much as he did.

Once he went go-carting. Jake and Junior arranged an afternoon when the track was typically closed to give Sammy free rein over a go-cart. Wearing a driver's helmet, Sammy roared around the track, bumping and turning and slamming into any immovable object. After thirty minutes he was worn out, and Junior particularly was reminded of Sammy's overindulgence of chocolate milk years earlier and was afraid that the rough ride might cause Sammy to have a convulsion. Instead, all the way back to the center that day he talked about his afternoon with Fireball Roberts. As he told the story, Sammy asked Jake to guess how fast he was going. Jake knew that if he guessed anything less than 120 miles per hour, he would get a disgusted reaction from Sammy. This time he said,

"Sammy, I believe you told me this story once before, and I think you said you were going seventy-five miles an hour. Were you really going that fast?"

Sammy slapped his fist on the front seat and replied, "You know better than that. I was going a hundred twenty-five miles per hour! That's faster than Daddy ever went!" The brothers' lighthearted teasing never stopped.

Sammy's only priority in life was to make a daily visit to see Mama. Although she was living in a subliminal state, he sat beside her and played his harmonica. On other days he just talked to her about their times together, just as they used to do on the porch. Once after he had been with her all afternoon, Mama extended her hand and gently squeezed Sammy's hand. It was her final expression of love to anyone. "I love you, Mama," Sammy whispered. Two days later,

Mama passed away. Her death was expected and a blessing. Sammy never again visited in the wing where her room had been located.

After he turned sixty-six, Sammy's strength began to diminish. He stopped traveling the halls. His appetite faded, and his vigor for living left him.

Junior visited with Sammy every day for the last month of his life, and Jake came by several times a week. On his last visit, Jake brought him a chocolate milk shake, his favorite. Sammy took a small swallow and pushed the rest away. The three brothers sat together all afternoon and into the evening, but shortly before midnight, Jake prepared to leave.

"Sammy, can I do anything for you before I go?" he asked.

Sammy nodded weakly. He pointed to the dresser next to the bed. There bound in leather were two books. One was Miss Mamie's Slim Sam book, and the other was Mama's Bible.

"Would you like for us to read?" Junior asked. Sammy nodded and pointed to Jake, who held the Slim Sam book.

"Do you want me to read the whole book?" Jake teased.

A thread of a smile came on Sammy's lips as he indicated, "No."

Slowly Jake read through many of the titles without a reaction until he came to "Campin' Out." Sammy motioned to stop. Then Jake began reading:

Campin' Out

It was a mild Autumn day when little Sam went
Out in the woods with his small canvas tent.

He'd heard campin' was a whole lot of fun
And he'd be huntin' and fishin' with his pole and pop gun.

For a while it went well, but no fish did he get
And things seemed to change about the time the sun set.
It was dark with no moon when he heard a faint hoot,
And he grabbed his pop gun and got ready to shoot.

When the sound came no more he heard himself say,
"This gun did the trick cause it scared them away."
In a moment or two he started to think
That he'd forgotten his food and his water to drink.

With no food or water, he decided to doze
When he heard a faint tickling on the end of his nose,
He slapped it away, but soon he could hear
A buzzing mosquito quite close to his ear.

"I don't like this," cried Sam, "and I can't really see
Why campin' is all it's cracked up to be.
With a rock for a cushion and dirt for a bed,
I want my old bunk and a pillow for my head."
Sam packed up his gear, left the woods toward his lawn.
Good news, thought Sam, *Mama left the light on.*

Jake closed the book. Sammy smiled and pointed to Junior.

Junior held one of Mama's leather Bibles. It was one of the sixteen
worn and heavily marked Bibles in her library. The book marker had
been placed in the book of John 14:2–3.

Sammy whispered the words as Junior began to read.

"In my Father's house are many mansions: if it were not so, I would have told you. I go to prepare a place for you. And if I go and prepare a place for you I will come again and receive you unto myself; that where I am, there ye may be also."

Junior closed the Bible and placed his hand on Sammy's hand. Jake stood at the door for a while and then slipped quietly away. Junior stayed almost until dawn before going home.

The next morning the boys fully expected to hear that Sammy had passed away during the night. Instead, the message from the nurses' station said that Sammy was awake and wanted Junior to bring him a breakfast from Beck's Restaurant. Junior would know what to bring. Around eleven o'clock with Junior's assistance, Sammy was doing his best to consume some scrambled eggs, sausage, and grits.

In a voice slightly stronger than a whisper, Sammy said, "Junior, last night I had a dream. I could see myself crossing a bridge. It was easy for me because now I was healthy and strong. On the other side I saw Mama encouraging me onward. And I saw Miss Mamie. She was smiling. And there was Daddy waving with one hand and holding little Putter in the other. It was a beautiful place in my dream. *Finally*, I thought to myself, *I am normal*. Then, as I hurried toward the family, my dream ended, and I woke up."

Junior moved closer and laid both hands on Sammy. One hand was on Sammy's hand, and the other was on his chest. Sammy closed his eyes, as if to rest. While he took two or three deep, deliberate breaths, Junior quietly said, "Sammy, that was not a dream. That was a vision of the place where you will be someday, maybe today."

In a moment Sammy was gone.

Junior sat quietly with Sammy for a few minutes. There was no rush to call the nurses. He was now in heaven and in a much happier place with those whom he loved. Junior prayed words of thanksgiving and slowly covered Sammy with the bed sheet. Tired though he was, Junior was relieved.

The funeral was uplifting. Family, friends, distant relatives, strangers, staff members from the center, and even one from Chestnut Grove were in attendance. There were some tears, but the tears were overshadowed by the celebration of a life patiently lived a day at a time, often in difficult and troubled circumstances.

His tombstone where he was laid to rest was situated between Mama and Putter. It read:

Francis Samuel Lamb
    "Sammy"
Born: February 22, 1931
Died: October 27, 1997

In my Father's house are many mansions.
If it were not so, I would have told you.
I go to prepare a place for you
So that where I am, there you may be also.

The crowd departed, but Junior, Jake, and their families lingered to pay their last respects. As the two remaining Lamb families rode away together in the limousine, Jake's daughter was reading through the registry of guests who attended the funeral and asked, "Who is Callie T? Was she here?"

"Callie Cross was Sammy's best friend when they were in school together at Chestnut Grove School in the mountains," Jake explained.

"Was it kinda like college?" his daughter asked.

"No, it was more like a church-sponsored education center for people who had developmental needs like Sammy."

"Was Callie his girlfriend?"

"I don't know for sure because Sammy never told me. But I do know this—Callie cared about Sammy for her entire life, and a person like that is a very special friend."

"One last question, Daddy. One last question. Do you think they will see each other in heaven?"

"Yes, I do, honey. I really believe they will."

"Daddy, Daddy. Look at this. There was someone at the funeral named Benjamin Franklin. Do you know him?"

"Yes, I do. He came to my father's funeral, too. He owned a restaurant near Bostic. Honey, haven't I told you that story?"

"No, I don't think so."

"Well, let me tell you about the first time Sammy and our family met Benjamin Franklin. We had just made our first visit to Chestnut Grove School in the edge of the mountains, and on the way back home we stopped for supper at Mr. Franklin's restaurant. We were all in a happy mood, and we all were hungry. The restaurant was small and crowded, and no sooner had we gotten our order than Sammy ..."

The End

EPILOGUE

Unbeknownst to the forebearers who in the 1880s determined the site for Willow Springs Cemetery, the burial grounds had been located atop a layer of sedimentary limestone that, throughout history, had protected a hollow underground chamber. Twelve years after Sammy's death, and following a four-day period of torrential rains, a portion of the cemetery, including the Lambs' graves, collapsed into a thirty-five-foot sinkhole.

Damages to Sammy's casket required that it be replaced. Among his remains were dust, a skeletal system, remnants of clothing, one silver ring, two gold class rings, and one small cherry seed.

APPENDIX

Miss Mamie's Notebook

The Trials and Tribulations of Slim Sam Flimflamigen

Introduction

Samuel David Flimflamigen, Junior was his real name,
But as a child, Slim Sam was who he became.

All skin and bones but a nice little kid,
He always got it wrong, no matter what he did.

He was awkward and clumsy and didn't have a clue
Of what was the proper or best thing to do.

He was vulnerable and funny, a unique little boy,
And here are his stories for all folks to enjoy.

Big Boy's Gun

When Slim Sam was seven, he thought it'd be fun
If Santa would bring him a real BB gun.
He'd asked Santa before, but never received,
But this year was different—he *really* believed.

Christmas came in the night, and Sam crept out of bed.
He thought from his window he had seen Santa's sled
Zooming next door quite low in the sky.
He was sure it was Santa, 'cause only his sled can fly.

Sam eased down the hall. He barely could see,
For a really dark house is as dark as can be.
He squinted his eyes as he peeked in the den
And looked toward the chimney where Santa had been.

It was the dim reflection from an outside light
That caused Sam to think that he really might
Have spied his gun underneath the big tree.
For sure, thought Sam, *it's a Red Ryder BB.*
Morning came slowly, then the first rays of sun
Revealed for certain Sam had his new gun.
I'm so glad it's Christmas, Sam thought with great joy,
'Cause Santa really knows that I'm a big boy.

Smart Hoppy Toad

One day Sam was walking down the road
When he spotted a big brown hoppy toad.

That critter was as fat as any Sam'd seen
But he wasn't afraid, 'cause toads aren't that mean.

Sam thought he would catch him and put him in his box,
The one with air holes and two tight locks.

The toad seemed to know what was in Sam's soul
'Cause he jumped inside a dark stump hole.

Sam reached into that dirty black muck,
And before he knew it, his arm got stuck.

He'd been caught by a root, and his fingers got numb,
And worst of all, he'd been embarrassingly dumb.

'Cause that toad came out on the far side of the stump,
And away he bounded with a thumpty, thump, thump.

It's a bad, bad day for a boy, it's true,
To think that a hoppy toad is smarter than you.

Winter Lake

Slim Sam Flimflamigen thought he would take
His first skating jaunt across an ice-covered lake.

At first he knew that he was fond
Of gliding along on this quaint little pond.

But about the time he turned to go back,
He noticed a small zigzagging ice crack.

Slim Sam knew for sure there was danger ahead
And that the ice all around him was something to dread.

The ice gave way, and with a bone-chilling thud,
His feet hid the bottom of slushy, cold mud.

Shaking and quivering, he got out okay,
But the following words were all he could say.

"In the future I know I'd bbetter think ttwice
Bbefore I sstep out on a ssheet of tthin ice."

Tree Hole

Slim Sam Flimflamigen was telling me
That not long ago he saw a hole in a tree.

Not worried one bit, he thought he'd find
If anything was hidden in that gnarled old pine.

He leaned way over and got down on one knee
And looked inside quite stealthfully.

He thought he might find an old treasure chest.
What he didn't expect was a bumblebee's nest.

Those bees stung him twice before he could think.
His blue eyes looked weird in six shades of dark pink!

Slim Sam Flimflamigen was a poor sight to see
'Cause one eye was fatter than the hole in the tree.

When asked what he learned from his careless mistake,
Sam said, "Bee holes can give you an awful headache."

Trappin'

One day when his Grandpaw was takin' a nap,
Slim decided to set a killer mouse trap.
Not long before they had seen a mouse
Dartin' around in their old log house.

The last time they had seen him was under the bed
Where Pawpaw had just laid his sleepy old head.

Slim got out a trap and added some cheese,
Not aware that Grandpaw was ready to sneeze.

Slim slid that trap so no mouse could hear
Right next to Pawpaw's enormous right ear.

About that time Gramps let out his sneeze
And fell out of bed and down to his knees.

The grip on his ear was as tight as a vice,
And he thought he'd been caught by a rat or five mice!

The trap broke his ear right straight down the middle,
And now oddly enough his big ear looked little.

That ear flopped around like the ears on their pup.
One ear flipped down, and the other stuck up.

Slim knew from the start he had done something bad,
'Cause no one would look at the ears on Granddad.

Fire Ants

When Sam sprained his ankle, he found it much
Easier to walk if he carried a crutch.
One day he was out just taking a stroll
When his crutch sank down into a fire ants' hole!

Those ants came out as mean as could be,
And the first sting he felt was below his left knee.
Before he knew it, they covered both feet,
And in less than a second, all he felt was hot heat.

When he yanked out his crutch, he fell in the sand,
And then he saw them all over his crutch hand.
He got to his knees to try to avoid those mean ants
When he felt those devils inside his short pants!

Folks still remember that hot summer's day. They'd never heard
anyone holler that way.

Stuck in Glue

One day Slim Sam put on his left shoe
After filling it half full of sticky white glue.

His shoe had been loose and didn't feel right,
But in just a few minutes his foot was stuck tight.

He yanked, and he pulled, but it held like a lock.
In appearance it looked like an odd-shaped white rock.

To get his foot free took nine days, maybe ten,
And Sam knew not to do that ever again!

Deaf Sam

Slim Sam Flimflamigen had no fear
When his thumb got stuck in his left ear.

"It's like the day, I suppose,
When two toes got stuck inside of my nose.

I got some pepper and sprinkled it about,
And after a while I sneezed them out!"

Not thinking too clearly, Sam did something dumb
And crammed his right ear with this other free thumb.

Then both thumbs got stuck, and it's painfully clear
That Sam couldn't hear nothin' out of either ear.

The good news was that when his folks yelled at him,
He couldn't hear a word from any of them.

Skunk in Bunk

When Slim Sam Flimflamigen was just a boy,
Goin' to camp was usually a joy.
The campers would run, climb, swim, and play.
They'd go from sunup til the end of the day.

At night they would sit by the fire until late
And hear scary stories that little kids hate.
'Cause going to bed is not any fun
When a spook can fly faster than a camper can run.

But Slim Sam was special … he was eight years old.
He was fearless and brave and admirably bold.
One night after the boys had warmed their cold toes
A stinky, odd smell passed through each camper's nose.

They'd just begun to hop in their bunk
When out popped the head of a black-and-white skunk.
Sam grabbed that skunk by his black-and-white hide,
Ran to the door, and heaved him outside.

Now the question remains if you're an eight-year-old hunk,
How do you handle a stinkin' old skunk?
Do you run out the door like a wise kid should do
Or smell like Slim Sam for a week, maybe two?

First Love

In the third grade Sam really liked school
'Cause when it was over, he'd go to the pool.
Some kids made fun because he was slim.
"Ostrich legs" was the name big bullies called him.

But the taunting stopped when they saw Sam swim.
In fact, they had admiration for him.
He could swim back and forth at a rapid, smooth pace.
He was fast, so fast, he could win a fish race.

One day while doing a few laps on his back,
He saw a new girl who was as slim as a tack.
"It's love at first sight," he knew as she passed.
"She'll be my sweetheart—my first and my last."

But a strange thing happened on that pool swimming day.
Poor Sam couldn't think of a thing he could say. His small heart
pounded. His head turned with a jerk,
But try as he did, his mouth would not work.

He even gulped water, which he'd never done before,
As the girl of his dreams walked toward the end door.
Before the first wave of sadness hit Slim,
She said, "Slim Sam, could you teach me to swim?"

Printed in the United States
By Bookmasters